MW00588626

Vince Guerra

BEYOND

THE

GOLDEN HOUR

Vince Guerra

Author photo by LaCroix Photography
Edited by Full Spectrum Editing
Cover by Jake Libby
Library of Congress Control Number: 2018951696

Printed in the United States of America

Published by Copperlight Wood
PO Box 870697
Wasilla, AK 99687
copperlightwood.com

ISBN 978-1-7325719-0-7

Vince Guerra

AUTHOR'S NOTE

Like most young men, I grew up fascinated with battle. My father's generation grew up with John Wayne and Steve McQueen; my generation was raised on Harrison Ford and Tom Cruise. War and the fictionalized depiction of battle was entertaining. It wasn't until the first Gulf War that I began to see the reality of service and sacrifice with my own eyes – it was my generation's first war, and we had no clue it was just the beginning of what was to come. I vividly remember my sister honking her horn in support of the troops at yellow-ribbon adorned intersections from 1990-1991. I was fifteen years old.

Over the next decade I devoured military fiction and non-fiction accounts of the Second World War and Vietnam. I looked into the possibility of becoming an Army helicopter pilot. But for all of the fascination and respect I had for these men and women in uniform, I never made the decision to serve myself.

After 9/11 there were many moments when I wondered if I should have joined. I had a wife and one-year old, but so did many men who were at that moment answering the call. I decided to remain home and support the troops as best I could.

In researching this book I gained insight into just

how much I don't know. And though I believe what I've written holds up to the spirit of what these warriors do in the real world – drawing heavily on non-fiction accounts of real life situations – I have no delusions that my story is anything more than fiction.

To veterans who read this, please know that in writing this story I have tried to honor what you do. And where I may have failed in realism, I hope to measure up in respecting what you've done and the sacrifices you and your family have made to protect mine. Thank you.

Beyond the Golden Hour

CONTENTS

PROLOGUE

There is no sense of smell in a dream. Aiden McCoy's parents told him this at an early age, and it was as they said. He had never smelled anything in a dream. For this reason, the scent of a damp wood pile in mid-fall — usually so fragrant and comforting — was now terrifying him. He could smell, and so this must not be a dream. For the rest of his life, Aiden would remember every detail of the most awful day of his young life; this day on which he sat like a stone in the familiar woods while his hero lay bleeding to death before his wide blue eyes.

———

Aiden and Josiah spent most of their childhood playing around the woodpile. Metal dump trucks that perfectly fit Aiden's toddler backside — propelled by his older brother Josiah — bounced over broken tree branches and wood chips in this dirt. Five-foot high walls of stacked logs served as forts in the winter, makeshift battlements in snowball fights. Six kids grew up in these woods. They worked and played here. They watched their father split logs by the hundred, mesmerized, watching lumber snap and shoot out to the right and left, delighting the destructive appetite of the boys in particular. From the first, both boys longed to wield this power.

First Josiah, and later Aiden, lobbied their father for the chance to take a swing with the maul. Dad called it an ax, but it was really a maul. Calling it an ax was easier than explaining the difference, but as they grew older and became more interested in tools and equipment, their father elaborated, saving detail for more serious inquiries. Dad's first priority concerning tools as well as everything else, was to instill proper respect. The garage was a treasure trove of dangerous tools, few more so than the maul.

While similar to an ax, the maul has more inherent destructive potential. Essentially a sledgehammer, yet pointed on one end, it is heavy, small, and exceedingly powerful. Perfectly designed to slice through heavy chunks of wet wood with minimum effort. The weight of the tool, its design, and the requisite force applied by its user will shatter anything that falls under its weight. This was the reason their father was reluctant to allow the boys to swing it.

Josiah was fifteen by the time he was finally allowed to use the maul independently. It made him feel manlier than any of the other tasks he enjoyed, quickly learning the reason his dad relished splitting wood. A method for unleashing aggression, masked as productivity. There was no desire to step up to the chainsaw; partially intimidation, but mainly because cutting up logs was a lot harder than splitting them. Now a seasoned veteran,

Josiah split logs occasionally for fun, sometimes because he was asked, or on days like today, as penance.

This particular trip to the woodpile was precipitated by a wrestling match that began in their bunk beds but surreptitiously spread to other rooms and tragically ended with an impact upon little sister's eye, and all before 7 am— which to Mom was the greater crime. House banishment was swift, but there were worse punishments, and, with teamwork they managed to have a fairly productive morning. Aiden set logs on the stump for Josiah to split, then gathered the expelled pieces, stacking them between two nearby spruce trees.

Late August was cold, and the ground wet with seasonal rain, making the footing unstable. Gloved hands gripped the maul with slightly less friction. Hard work for tough boys who didn't mind. The mosquitoes were dying off, and the sun was out. All in all, it was a fine way to spend a morning; that is, until Josiah missed.

Josiah had been struggling with a particularly thick, wet log with a 14-inch diameter. He didn't miss the log completely, just the center. That, or the blade had come down slightly tilted rather than straight. Regardless, the result was the same.

Three successive swings ended with a spine-jarring thud. The maul was firmly implanted in the wood, forcing him to wrench it out, wiggling the handle and applying leverage to free it. Frustration commenced its assault on concentration, eliminating patience. A fourth swing, rushed, with even greater force, and worse footing due to haste and outright anger.

As he brought it down with a growl the maul skimmed off the edge of the log, slamming into Josiah's left calf. Mercifully not a head-on impact that would have shattered his shin, but the blow did plenty of damage to its credit, digging a deep gash into the muscle beside the bone.

Three things happened in a flash. Josiah let out a hoarse cry, fell over on his side, and instinctively grabbed his leg as blood began to appear between his fingers. Aiden heard the cry but didn't see the impact as his back was turned.

What he might have seen when he turned to face his brother — now on the ground, reeling in pain and holding his leg— was an emergency requiring swift attention. But that's not what Aiden saw. All he saw was blood, lots of blood, more than he had ever seen in his life, and it turned him to stone. He registered Josiah's voice imploring him to get Mom, but Aiden couldn't. He was immobilized, scared, watching his brother bleed to death.

There was so much blood. He couldn't take his eyes off of it. As he stood paralyzed with fear, it was all he could think about: fast at first, but now slowly oozing out of his brother's leg. Everything inside of him said he should get up and run for help. Call out to his mom, his sister, anyone.

Had he been able to make the attempt, Aiden would have discovered his voice was as dysfunctional as the rest of his faculties. He was conscious of what he was seeing, knew what needed to be done, but was incapable. It was maddening, terrifying. He tried to speak but his lips and tongue seemed glued shut.

He tried to stand but his legs would not respond. He wanted to wave his hands but his arms shook. The entire scene seemed to be occurring in a different place, as if he was watching it on a screen, and then, as if to jolt him back to reality, his nose betrayed the hope that this was all a bad dream, a nightmare that he might wake up from. He smelled the blood.

The intense, sickening, metallic smell of blood, his older brother's blood, seeping into the dirt. The odor of the sticky red liquid mingled with sawdust and it was a new, awful sensation. Familiar smells were there, too: the wet, decaying, spotted birch leaves that usually indicated winter's too-fast approach.

The smoke from the neighbor's woodstove wafted down to him from a couple of acres away. Mom's freshly baking bread a few dozen feet away, being prepared for a lunch that Josiah may never see.

Help me Mom, his ten-year-old heart cried out, unassisted by his vocal cords. He would have cried but apparently his tear ducts were not functioning either. He was in a silent box, unable to move, hardly able to think, certainly unable to speak, and mercilessly, unable to wake up from this nightmare.

Call for Mom, he thought. He tried to scream but his lips couldn't make the sound. *Run for Mom*, the inner voice suggested. He tried to stand up from his kneeling position, but his legs began to shake. *Oh, God.*

He watched for what seemed like an eternity. Eyes and mouth wide open, his heart dying while his brother's blood spread wider across the sawdust and dirt.

Everyone has a defining moment. Some have many, but everyone has at least one event they can pinpoint which influenced their decisions from that moment forward, changing the course of more lives than their own. For many people the moment is one of great pain, and they yearn to go back in time and alter it — yet it continues to taunt them in quiet moments of the years that follow. Some stir the spirit and provide encouragement to seek out more and better rewards, as a child who finds a four-leaf clover spends the rest of the summer expectantly eying every clover patch from then on. A defining moment could be the stinging rebuttal from an insecure or cruel person, or the crushing blow of an unexpected death that sucks the drive right out of you. We never know what the catalyst for our moment will be.

This was Aiden's defining moment, as life drained from his brother's leg.

Fortunately, the boys were blessed with a twelve-year-old sister, Alyse, born with razor-sharp discernment, strong nerve, and an exceedingly loud voice. And though she was accustomed to seeing her brothers on the ground, bleeding even, she was certainly not accustomed to seeing them unconscious.

Her eyes briefly took in the scene. "Josey?" she asked meekly.

One look at Aiden and she realized the futility of seeking assistance from him. Instead, she did as ten-year-old girls are wont to do, and yelled as loud as she could.

"Mom!"

And then she was off, a mad dash to the house, one hundred feet in mere seconds, flying through the back door, screaming as muddy bare feet smeared over wood floorboards.

"Mom! Josiah is bleeding!"

A mother of six children does not easily lose her composure, nor often transition to triage mode at a child screaming downstairs, even a bleeding one. Parents have an internal assessment that translates screams and categorizes them by severity. Alyse's scream rated on the high end, and the accompanying exclamation heightened the alert status.

"I think he passed out!" Alyse said.

Alyse, having set an Olympic record with her dash to the house, was outdone by Mom, who, leaving a toddler to her own devices on the toilet seat upstairs, set another record with her dash to the woodpile — flying through the house, down the stairs, out the back door, across the lawn, till she came upon the ghastly scene.

Unhesitating, in a swift motion she stripped off her beloved hoodie and put pressure upon the gushing wound. She ran through the mental checklist as her brain processed what was, and what ought, to be happening, and began a dialogue with herself.

Josey's unconscious.

Is he breathing?

Yes. Thank God.

Bleeding?

Yes.

Compress the wound. How much blood is he losing, has he lost?

Hard to tell.

"Aiden how long has he been out." She asked without asking, and looked at Aiden, who was as still as a lawn ornament.

"Aiden!" she snapped before registering the terror in her younger son's eyes. Filing away the concern for Aiden for another day, she turned back to Josiah, the priority patient. The dialogue continued.

Tourniquet?

Not necessary. More pressure.

Still unconscious. He needs blood to his heart. Elevate his legs. Phone?

"Aiden, get the phone!"

Aiden jolted awake, and found in his mother's strength the ability he lacked on his own. It was a sensation not unlike when your ear finally pops after having a cold for several days. The immense clarity that overwhelms your sense of hearing is dramatic, somewhat frightening, and always a relief. Aiden was back, and he was able to stand though his legs were still shaky. Still, he had a direction and meant to execute it.

The spell was broken.

He turned, stumbled over a split log, got up and struggled on all fours. As he scrambled toward the house he was almost bowled over by Alyse, who already had the phone in her hand and was dialing 911.

Defeated, Aiden shrank back toward the side of the house and stood watching, out of the way of people who weren't...worthless. From a distance he watched as if seeing a scene on TV: Mom in control, Alyse keeping pressure on the wound, Mom reviving Josiah. The TV was on mute. No sound penetrated his increasing sense of guilt.

It's taking so long.

Aiden's heart briefly allowed him to find relief when Josiah came to, and tried to sit up, but dread triumphed again when Josiah swiftly threw up.

What's going to happen to him?

Aiden was forgotten in the mayhem. Nobody noticed him shrinking farther and farther away. Someone finally hollered and ordered him to get in the car to follow Josiah's ambulance to the hospital. Aiden was hardly noticed in the waiting room when Dad arrived.

Aiden looked at his shoes for the awful duration, didn't respond when his mother, now able to address the pained eyes she witnessed earlier, put her arm around him and spoke words of affirmation. He heard his parents loving words, but his own thoughts were louder, clearer, and contrastingly condemning.

Three hours and fifteen stitches later, they were all home. Josiah sat on the couch, blissfully eating Chinese take-out and enjoying his first experience with painkillers. Dad had insisted they needed to celebrate Josiah being okay, and they could do it more properly now before the ER and ambulance bills arrived in the mail. It also tempered the three-year-old's agitation at having been forgotten on the upstairs potty for twenty minutes.

The doctor had assured them it wasn't the blood loss that had caused Josiah to pass out, but the pain and shock. The wound was deep and the blood made it appear deadly. The real danger was infection and not keeping a fifteen-year-old off his feet in the waning days of fall.

"Let it heal and he probably won't even miss any hockey this year," the doctor assured them.
Hearing all of this relieved Aiden for Josiah's sake, but did nothing to assuage his self-imposed humiliation. His brother had needed him. He had failed. There was no way around that. When he finally mustered up the courage to approach the couch and apologize to Josiah, he was given a dismissive wave.

"It's all right, you couldn't have really done anything, and besides it was no big deal. Don't worry about it, Aiden."

Josiah was the rational sort. But all Aiden heard was, "You couldn't do a thing."

Later that night, lying in bed, Aiden mulled over the terrible memory. Somewhere around 9:00 p.m. he set aside the shackles of guilty condemnation, and welcomed resolve in its place. He scanned the books on his bedside shelf, landed on a rarely used Boy Scout's handbook and flipped it open to the first-aid section. Neither brother had been a Boy Scout, but they had the manuals nonetheless, among the countless volumes of a variety of topics, and the handbook was full of good information.

Dad had bought two of them at a thrift store for fifty cents. They were vintage, full-color printings from the 1950s with many pages falling out. The age was irrelevant since the information didn't really change, plus it satisfied one of Mom and Dad's sacred principles: the older the book, the better it usually is. It sat on the shelf as reference and had gathered dust up to this point, a mere curiosity. Now Aiden devoured it, reading and re-reading sections. He made mental notes and asked a hundred questions in his mind, determined to have them answered in the morning. He fell asleep with the light on while searching his armpits for pressure points, too tired to turn the lamp off before finally closing his eyes.

Around midnight their father walked in to check on Josiah and tuck in his boys, relieved over the outcome. He noticed Aiden, asleep with the book resting face-down on his chest, still opened. He picked it up to close it, and was a little surprised at the content on the page. Lacerations, splints, tourniquets, etc…he looked back at Aiden, wondering what must have been going on inside Aiden's little mind to cause him to spend several hours studying first aid. He closed the book, set it down next to Aiden, stroked his son's soft red hair, and turned off the lamp.

It was the first time Aiden read over fifty pages in one night.

Beyond the Golden Hour

Part I

1

POLARIS

17:00:00
Afghanistan, 2003

Bullets chipped away at the rock wall above and behind their heads, AK-47 rounds splitting the air and ricocheting around the canyon. After returning fire for several minutes, the five special operators were still without casualties, but the rate of fire was increasing and they were running a higher and higher risk of getting bogged down. Moving positions twice while picking off enemies, they had managed to maintain initiative. Mortar rounds began to fall, inaccurate but soon to be adjusted. They were running out of room in the narrow canyon to fall back. They needed more firepower. They needed help out of this mess.

Andy was already in contact with air assets, having whipped out his radios as soon as the first shots rang out. Now he was ready to order in the first airstrike of the battle. All he needed was the go-ahead from the mission leader, Porter, who had his hands full knocking off bad guys wherever they popped their heads up.

The assortment of radios and batteries an Air Force Combat Air Controller — CCT — has are arguably more valuable than any other weapon on the battlefield. Andy's radios represented an incalculable amount of firepower, linking soldiers on the ground with the combined air forces of the western world and all they could bring to bear. His value was not lost on the four Navy SEALs with whom he had been living, concealed on this mountain for the past ten days.

They had protected him and grown to respect him, not only for his grit but also for his uncanny aptitude for navigation. He had become the pathfinder and always managed to get them to their waypoint on schedule and without obstacle, until now. Concealed and low behind the rocks, he kept an eye on Porter and waited.

"Light up that ridge!" Lt. Porter said, pointing in the direction of the mortar's position.

Andy gave a thumbs-up and began speaking to whomever he could find on the other end of the radio. He was in his element, years of specialized training in the California desert guiding his actions automatically, essentially the equivalent of a civilian air traffic controller. While someone managing the airspace in the civilian world is mostly concerned with ensuring the blips on his screen reach their destinations without colliding, CCTs orchestrate which ones get to blow stuff up.

There is a verbal shorthand used among pilots and controllers that ensures messages don't get lost in translation, time and fuel aren't squandered, pilots know what to expect, and in combat, that the wrong people don't die.

Of course in war, the wrong people often die, disproportionately as a result of friendly fire and most frequently at the hands of aircraft providing close air support. The phrase troops in contact means close contact with the enemy. Troops in close contact are equally subject to aircraft delivering the bombs. In decades past, bombs fell wherever the wind took them with relatively little able to be done to direct them once released. The skill of the pilots in those days was every bit as essential as it is today; however, the modern battlefield is blanketed with technology that tries to take luck out of the equation.

Every square foot of terrain is detailed on computer mapping, separated into grids, stored in computers on handheld devices by the ground troops, and in the weapons systems of multi-million-dollar (sometimes multi-billion-dollar) aircraft in the air.

Troops on the ground, under fire, stressed and disoriented and desperate, communicate with cool men in fancy machines and hopefully agree on which pieces of dirt need to explode. CCTs are the variable that save lives, ensuring the best available aircraft uses the proper weapon on the right target in time and with frequency. Failing this has caused many a combat pilot incalculable heartache. There are few tragedies in war equal to killing one's allies. Andy's main job was to see that this didn't happen.

Andy's preference would have been an AC-130U Spooky gunship, a newer version of the converted AC-130 Spectre gunship that incorporated a single 25mm Gatling gun. The large imposing aircraft could slowly circle the ground target firing 1800 rounds per minute. Andy had two in the vicinity. One was on alert, about thirty minutes away on the ground. The other was airborne and closer, but would need to meet up with an aerial refueling tanker before it could commit to join the fight. Andy mentally fixed this as plan B, which would be great thirty minutes from now but would do nothing to keep them alive in the meantime.

He scrutinized other available aircraft. There was a B-1 bomber heading nearly overhead in a couple of minutes with plenty of bombs. This he wrote off as no good. The five men on the ground were too closely engaged with the enemy for that kind of a strike. Andy wanted guns to strafe the ridgeline, and didn't have time to set up the target for a precision-guided bomb strike.

There were a pair of F-16s that could push afterburners and arrive in about five minutes, but they were so low on fuel they would only be able stay on station for a matter of minutes. Again, not optimal. It turned out that his best option was a pair of A-10 Warthogs returning from a mission, and he could task at least one of them to head this direction.

It had been flying a perimeter guard while its wingman made several runs on ground targets, burning through practically all of its weapons and most of its fuel. The A-10 flying perimeter had endured watching all the action, itching to get into the fray, and was fully loaded with its weapons payload of AGM-65 Maverick missiles, 2.75-inch rockets, and its most devastating weapon, the 30mm Gatling cannon, capable of expending 3,900 uranium-depleted rounds per minute. The A-10's cannon was designed to destroy enemy armor, tanks, and vehicles. Its effect was not unlike spraying the ground with a pressure washer; everything disintegrated under its force.

The "Hog" was the preeminent ground support fighter and was exactly what Polaris needed. Andy called it in, counting off the time required to get them overhead.

"Hog inbound, ten minutes," he shouted.

Porter had been firing methodically for minutes that seemed like hours. He did the mental calculations. *Hold on for ten minutes. Yeah, we can do that.* He looked to his teammates. To the left were Teddy, an intimidating hulk of a man, and Ray, the team sniper. Both had their hands full, but Teddy quickly turned, glanced back over his shoulder and gave a hurried thumbs-up.

On the right and slightly behind Porter crouched the fifth and last member of Polaris, Chris, who was known throughout the SEAL fraternity as Gator.

Ten minutes, thought Porter. *Just keep your men alive for ten minutes. After that we can move. Keep up the fire.* Porter was one of the best natural leaders the Navy possessed. He had survived combat in holes and swamps the world over and possessed a well-known resume of accomplishments, but like most men of his caliber, never mentioned them. Still, everyone who served under or over him considered themselves fortunate, not least because most who did, lived. Porter intended that this mission would be no different.

Polaris had spent ten days reconnaissance on this particular mountain prior to command aborting the position. The five man team was ordered to extract at 2100. Given the distance they had to descend to reach the designated landing zone, it was clear that the team would be required to move out in daylight, and Porter had given the order reluctantly.

They would have much preferred to move at night for additional concealment. US special operators, on the ground or in the air, own the night, their most valuable tactical advantage. So far Polaris had not ventured about in daylight, making the initial trek up to the objective in the dead of night, and remained continuously concealed, except for some night reconnaissance around their hide by Gator in an attempt to locate alternate routes of attack and/or withdraw.

But time and weather were bad decision makers, and this time the threat of a significant snowstorm had forced the issue. It would shut down helicopter operations indefinitely, disrupt or outright sever communications, and thus render Polaris impotent. There was no point in keeping them there, and the window available to allow choppers in and out was diminishing. There was also a narrow list of appropriate landing zones, none of which were close. Knowing all of this and hearing the ticking clock in his head, Porter ordered the movement in broad daylight. Everyone knew it was the only option. Now they were paying for it.

Eight minutes now. Piece of cake, Porter convinced himself.

———

The A-10 pilot checked his weapons status and fuel. The former was fully loaded, the latter was reasonably adequate. He calculated distance to the target grid that the CCT on the ground had pinpointed. The pilot had done this hundreds of times, dozens of them in actual live fire combat situations.

As a U.S. Air Force Captain he had trained and executed close air support for more than ten years over multiple deployments and in several theatres, the mountains of Afghanistan in particular.

Pilots, especially fighter pilots, pride themselves in maintaining calm under pressure, but the weight of men under fire desperate for the support that only he was in a position to provide always humbled him and got him antsy. He wore it well, and by outward appearances one would never know how it galled him be patient while his multi-million-dollar aircraft approached the battlefield. *Almost there*, he said to himself, *Hang in there, gentlemen.*

—

Andy held up two fingers while looking to Porter. Two minutes. Polaris still had no casualties and plenty of ammo to hold off the erratic incoming fire, adequate cover for concealment from wildly inaccurate incoming mortar rounds, which would be corrected in time, though not likely within the next…minute and forty seconds.

For all the tenacity and breadth of weapons, jihadists had little quality training. Given even terms, the enemies of America were universally disadvantaged. But within the rocks and crags of their native territory, through superior numbers and the physics of terrain, they had been known to overwhelm the better equipped and vastly better-trained Coalition forces. Such are the realities of war. Minimizing the hazard with tactics honed from months of training,

Polaris literally kept a step ahead. Whenever a mortar round landed close, the team split in two different directions, Ray and Teddy moving one way, Andy, Porter, and Gator in another. Polaris, by falling back and dispersing twice, had revealed the mortar's exact position. This was Andy's primary concern and the first target on the Hog's agenda. A pilot's voice crackled on the radio.

"Polaris, this is Rapier-One-Seven. Approaching south of your position. Engaging target grid in thirty seconds."

Porter pulled the pin on a green smoke canister and tossed it into the clearing between him and the enemy. The pilot saw it through his heads-up display and immediately selected the most appropriate weapon given the tactical situation. The proximity of friendlies to the enemy was tricky; so was the rocky terrain that concealed men who the pilot knew were there but couldn't see. The heavy snow all around the ridges encircling the battlefield also caused additional visual uncertainty. Ruling out missiles entirely, he armed the 30mm cannon.

Andy had pinpointed two targets: a mortar team directly north of them, and a collection of riflemen in the rocks to their northeast. Additionally, Polaris was catching random small arms fire from the north and southeast. The Hog was going to be busy securing 270 degrees around Polaris, as they still needed a clear path to their landing zone.

A fortunate feature of the A-10's design was that it was incredibly quiet on approach and its victims rarely heard it before it was too late. Some enemies had designated it the "silent killer." It would be all over in a matter of minutes.

The men peeked over the rocks in anticipation, just enough to see the entire ridge become a huge cloud of snow, rocks, blood, and steel. The image was simultaneously terrifying and awesome.

As the enemy mortar fell silent, they heard the massive turbofan engines of the A-10 pulling up and banking to the right, soon to emerge from the rear of their position and take out target number two to the northeast. Andy was confirming the next target grid for the pilot as the enemy began firing wildly in all directions.

The operators didn't look behind them to see the

aircraft, instead keeping their attention on the remaining enemy, who now knew a U.S. fighter was about to engage them and began to scramble away. Polaris, ready to mow them down if necessary, knew the enemy couldn't outrun the Hog.

The 30mm cannon burped its devastating torrent, again producing a similar cloud of destruction. For a few seconds there was silence and Porter allowed himself a relieved breath, finally lowering his rifle for the first time in almost an hour. He instinctively looked up, straining to see the A-10 as it moved in and out of the growing and increasingly colorful clouds. The engine sounds reached their ears just as the fighter appeared on its bank to the right. He also saw a streak heading toward it.

Between the clouds, everyone had a perfect view of the aircraft as its right wing exploded and separated completely from the fuselage. Black smoke poured out of the A-10's missing wing, which flew away on its own trajectory. Disbelief mixed with rage as they watched the Hog spin out of control and dip behind the other side of the peak. A hundred ears across Afghanistan listened and reacted to what was said next.

"Mayday. Mayday. Mayday," followed by static, "Rapier-One-Seven. I'm hit… going down… punching out."

Thanks to the Hog, the road to the LZ was clear. Polaris had a helicopter to catch for home in five hours. In order to make it there in time for the exfil, they would have to move north immediately. There was no time to spare. The five men of Polaris stared at the empty patch of sun-setting sky where they had just seen the A-10 fall to pieces.

Nothing needed to be said. No order was given or sought. Polaris, a five-man team who wanted nothing more than to catch the next helicopter off this mountain — who, up to the last thirty seconds, were fixing to descend as fast as possible — now, instead, began the long and difficult climb back up in the direction they had just come.

A pilot was going down, and Polaris had no intention of waiting around for someone else to recover him. Assigning themselves a new mission, the SEALs were up and moving off long before Andy realized the fact. They were not going home.

Not without that pilot.

Vince Guerra

2

RAVEN

18:00:00
24th Special Tactics Squadron: Afghanistan

Aiden lay in his bunk immersed in twaddle. That was what his parents called it, twaddle: a particular caliber of book where depth is not requisite. Aiden had a passion, a love – not far removed from an addiction – for books. Not necessarily good ones, as evidenced by his current selection. He read upwards of thirty books a year, and over his six deployments had lost count of the total. He always brought some with him; the rest were sent by various familial suppliers, none more generous than his sister Alyse, who easily read twice his number annually.

His parents sent him and the other Pararescuemen in his unit care packages, filled with all variety of guy food, the necessities such as underwear, occasional extravagances such as a new set of headphones, and always a few books: something unique that his father recommended, or something that Aiden had requested. On a military base, in a warzone, those packages took on the same stature as a stocking on Christmas

morning, and were anticipated and devoured with equal
fervor and rapidity.

On a normal day, Aiden would read a book that
stretched him. But on returning from a particularly
disturbing mission, as he was today, some mindless
form of escape was in order.

All of the men in his unit had similar outlets; coping
mechanisms, tucked away on the little shelves next to
their bunks, makeshift plywood living quarters of
varying quality, the degree of which was entirely
dependent upon their commander's ability to fleece,
cajole, steal, or barter into requisition on their behalf
extravagances like doors, power, heaters, or adequate
lighting. War or no war, it was nice to have the
capability of sleep without shivering.

Air Force Pararescue Jumpers (PJs), the modern
battlefield's first responders, are constantly on high
alert, trained for a variety of missions, and ready for
anything that comes their way.

Any 12-hour shift could involve a mission of sorts,
maybe a sortie which is canceled at the last minute,
often a rapid insertion into an uncertain ground
situation, treating multiple casualties of varied severity,
patching them up however possible for evacuation,
utilizing complex medical procedures performed in the
back of a turbulent and cramped Blackhawk helicopter
to treat them, occasionally while getting shot at or
rolling around as the chopper pilots avoided ground-to-
air threats, and, ideally, handing off their patients to
surgeons at Coalition hospitals within one hour — the
golden hour — of the initial injury, since doing so
exponentially increases the odds of survival and
minimizes the likelihood of complications.

High-pressure jobs, especially ones where lives are
on the line, require an uncommon level of focus and a

penchant for creative determination. Aiden and his fellow PJs lived for it, but sustained over the course of days, weeks, and months, the stress would be unbearable but for the stringent training and room to decompress. Twaddle has its place, and Aiden read his book.

Yesterday's mission was brutal; child patients always are, not merely because treating them is so difficult technically, but because it is draining emotionally. A handful of times Aiden had treated Afghan children. He always immediately attached to them in a way he never did with grown men and women. Children injured in war, sometimes as a result of direct action, were simply tragic.

PJs were called in if the injury was a result of American ordnance. In that case, it would be their mission; if not, they would be ordered to stand down, and the child would die as Americans listened in frustration over the radio. In his combat experience, Aiden had saved one child, lost two others in the back of the chopper, and had no idea what had happened to the rest after he'd handed them off to the Afghan hospital. Part of him was grateful that he didn't know. Better a fantasy of victory than a dreaded reality.

Yesterday he and Hector had evacuated a beautiful seven-year-old girl missing an arm as a result of a bomb blast. She was stable, but had lost a ton of blood when the Raven chopper delivered her to the grateful doctors at the Afghan hospital. The chopper had quickly lifted off, with little more to offer than a goodbye look of concern. At least in the allied coalition hospital Aiden could take his patient all the way into the ER and give the doctors some background. But this was an Afghan patient, and the rules were different. He had no idea if this one had survived, either. The uncertainty weighed on him like someone sitting on his chest, but there was nothing he could do about it and he was past the point of second-guessing his actions.

"Hey, something's going on," Hector said as he peeked into Aiden's plywood cubicle, and without waiting for a reply, walked off toward the Tactical Operations Center.

Aiden dog-eared the page as he swung his legs off the bed and followed Hector down the hall toward the desk of the intelligence officer, where all the rest of Raven was gathered listening to the battle taking place over the radio. The PJs were always monitoring, waiting for a call to respond to. A ground casualty, a downed aircrew, an ejected pilot; any could require Raven's assistance and so they waited in silence, some with grim concern, some eating snacks, some fiddling with cans of wintergreen chewing tobacco…all waiting.

They watched the patchy images from the aerial drone, trying to make out land features and listening to the radio chatter of what seemed to be a pilot communicating with a CCT.

The pilot was speaking. "Polaris, this is Rapier-One-Seven. Approaching south of your position. Engaging target grid in thirty seconds."

Hector flashed a looked at Aiden who stood cold, emotionless, all concentration. Hector looked back, with increased interest. The rest of Raven carried on like normal, PJs, officers, and chopper pilots looked around the room the way people do when aching for more information but only getting it in disjointed doses.

They saw the first strike by the A-10's cannon, or rather the black-and-white disruption of the image indicating eliminated targets. A few muted exclamations uttered under breaths. Aiden merely looked ahead and said nothing.

The destruction was undeniable on the wall-mounted screens. Heads nodded in approval and everyone waited to hear what was going to happen next, most believing, all hoping, that the show was over, mercifully without casualties. Aiden waited.

The relief quickly gave way to shock as the pilot called out, "Mayday. Mayday.Mayday..."

A few seconds of horror transformed the room into complete silence; then, the calm, matter-of-fact voice of the pilot resumed.

"Rapier-One-Seven going down..."

"...punching out."

The word *mayday* was a catalyst. Every pair of eyes shifted, shoulders turned, men stepped to the wall of radios, listening in stunned silence to the pilot calmly and professionally telling the world that he was about to lose a multi-million-dollar aircraft, and possibly his life with it. Aiden was the exception.

He was already moving toward his gear when the pilot announced his intention to eject. The other members of Raven looked toward him only to see his back as he briskly led the way toward their next mission. Everyone scrambled after him.

—

The Raven pilots were behind the controls, warming up their choppers in mere minutes as the PJs grabbed the surplus gear required for what they anticipated to be the mission profile, brought it on board, and anticipated orders to lift off. The workhorse of the modern American military is the UH-60 Blackhawk helicopter or its variations, and it is the PJ's typical ride to work. Fast, durable, versatile, heavily armed, and, for this mission, grounded.

The location's elevation required MH-47 Chinooks. The Chinook, a twin-rotor, heavy-lift chopper had none of the flashy sex appeal of the Blackhawk. In football terms, if the Blackhawk is a running back, the Chinook is an offensive tackle: a gargantuan, plain-looking grunt who happens to be, like the Chinook, indispensable. Not much to look at, nor much fun to fly, but respected and reliable.

Chinooks have been in action since the Vietnam war, and prior to Afghanistan they were little more than a taxi or hauling service. The mountainous terrain of America's new theatre of battle changed its value overnight. High-altitude missions presented vast challenges in engine power, fuel consumption, and durability, and the Chinooks, the only choppers suitable for scaling the murderous mountain ranges, were perfectly suited for Afghanistan, much to the delight of their crew: a pilot, copilot, and three flight engineers, who doubled as door gunners on the side doors, and the back ramp.

It was clear that the recovery of Rapier-One-Seven required a high altitude insertion including four PJs to provide ground security and recovery; the Blackhawk simply wouldn't be able to make it up there. Flying a chopper into those mountains was hard enough — landing it safely with ten men, ammunition, and supplies, and taking on at least one more pilot, then getting enough power from the engines in thin air to carry them all to safety, was another matter entirely.

The Chinooks faced all the same challenges but with considerably better odds. The tradeoff was that Chinooks were loud and slow by comparison, with greater restrictions and more vulnerable to ground fire. But they could take a beating and keep airborne better than any chopper in the arsenal. There were always trade-offs.

Two Chinooks idled on the tarmac, rotor tips a few feet from each other. Twenty men on two helicopters sat in uncomfortable seats, waiting through a familiar delay, anxious as always but even more so today. Aiden sat in the back of the Chalk 2 bird, his crew a backup in case the lead chopper experienced difficulty, or worse. Aiden wanted to be on the ground for this mission, but mainly he just wanted to get that pilot up off the ground as fast as possible.

The lead bird would land and dispense four PJs, who would secure the landing zone, apprehend the downed pilot, treat any wounds he had, escort him back to the Chinook, and get the heck out of there, all in mere minutes, if not seconds. Aiden's bird would circle the landing zone, provide security from the air and intel on enemy movements, and wait in case the Chalk 1 bird got into trouble.

Rescuing a downed fighter pilot was the preeminent assignment, what every PJ wanted to do most, and for many of them it was the reason they chose to become PJs in the first place. Ninety percent of mission time was responding to medical emergencies, constantly flying all over Afghanistan pulling wounded or dying coalition and Afghan soldiers off the ground and whisking them away to NATO or Afghan hospitals with a speed and efficiency never matched in the history of warfare.

PJs go in armed for battle, but often never fire their weapons. Primarily trauma specialists, they spend the majority of their time practicing emergency medicine. They save lives every day, putting theirs on the line so that others may live.

They were moving now, speeding toward the distant

mountains. Aiden looked around at the other men in the chopper: three other PJs along with the flight crew, men he knew well, usually liked, and even loved at times. His eyes fell on Hector, who stared back, determined. Aiden looked away, went over the mission in his mind.

He longed for some kind of information, but so far all they knew was the general area where he went down. Any information about injuries or ground conditions would hopefully be forthcoming, but at present, there was none. He keyed his mic and asked their pilot how long till they were on station. The answer came back: approximately forty minutes.

Aiden leaned back. *Forty minutes.* He closed his eyes but wouldn't sleep. He never could sleep during the day, less so on a helicopter no matter how smooth the ride was, and this one was anything but. He wouldn't rest unless everything he could do was done, which meant he wouldn't sleep again until he was back on this chopper with the mission completed. He laid his head back against the web mesh seat. *Forty minutes.*

———

Aiden hadn't always wanted to be a PJ; he'd never even heard of them until he was seventeen. Like most young men he was preoccupied with the year ahead. Many men at that age vacillate between the trivial distractions common to their lifestyles while preparing future plans. This happens in direct proportion to their maturity and responsibility. Aiden had an abundance of both and was intentional in everything he did. Driven to succeed, he didn't waste time pursuing endeavors he had no intention of finishing. He researched how he wanted to spend the rest of his life with great calculation.

During his last year at home he came to realize he was dead set against college, and was kind of a jerk about it. It held absolutely no interest for him. The thought of spending hours on end, sitting in some overpaid professor's lecture was quite possibly the worst hell he could imagine for himself. He'd been inoculated to the college lecture hall as a visiting high school student enduring a semester of AP psychology, and simply did not understand what lectures had to do with the pursuit of knowledge that could be obtained, unfiltered, by reading. His parents' attempts to explain the benefits of listening to others' experience fell on deaf ears. He felt college was a sort of waiting room; a place where one listlessly racks up debt and wastes precious time. Aiden didn't like to waste time, he wanted to save lives.

But Aiden loved to learn; he was a great student who just never fit well into a traditional classroom. His singular passion was emergency medicine. He studied anatomy, watched documentaries on the topic, and seriously considered becoming a medic for the Army. He'd briefly entertained nursing — ever so briefly, considering the college aspect — and had pretty much settled on firefighting. Some of his parent's friends were firefighters, and had encouraged him in the pursuit.

"You get to save lives and break stuff. What could be better?" one of his dad's friends argued. Aiden had toured stations and spent weeks studying the practice tests. He trained every day and was fully confident that he would breeze through the physical exams, all set to apply once his eighteenth birthday rolled around — until one day he noticed a book his dad was reading about PJs.

Aiden picked it up the moment his dad put it down

and finished it four hours later. "That others may live"
— he kept thinking about their motto all the rest of that
day. He threw away all of his fire department written
materials and went on a seven-mile run instead of his
usual five. When he returned, he'd decided he would be
a PJ, and two years later he was. Eight years after that,
he was sitting in the mesh seat of a Chinook, fighting
fear, and embarking on the most important mission of
his life.

———

Aiden reached into his pants pocket and pulled out a
PowerBar. His routine before hockey games had always
been to polish off a PowerBar thirty minutes prior to
face-off. It was a marker that mentally prepared him for
action. He sipped his water bottle and tried to clear his
head. No thoughts of home, or pointless distractions;
just blank rest and focus for the green light. He glanced
at his watch. *Twenty-three minutes.*

Aiden was not married, had no sweetheart at home,
nor any prospects of one. There were a half-dozen
young ladies in his social circle who would marry him if
he'd asked. He didn't date much. Dating
seemed…unnatural. He wanted something deeper. He
had grown up watching the way his grandfather looked
at his grandmother, and how his father looked at his
mother, and until he met the girl that caused him to feel
the way that they looked, he knew his time would be
better spent elsewhere. So he refused to lead girls on,
wouldn't waste their time, and left many puzzled and
heartbroken as a result. He figured he'd know her when
he saw her. He was intentional, and so he was single.

He looked at his watch again, realized he never did
that on other missions and silently admonished himself.

You need to relax. This is just another mission. Don't overthink it. That's how you screw up. He looked around. Just relax. He uttered a prayer that was at that moment, being echoed by dozens of men on the ground, and twenty men on two helicopters, *God, protect him. Hang on, we're coming for you.*

3

RAPIER

This was actually the third time he had dangled under the straps of a parachute. The first time, when he was eighteen, his father had miraculously convinced his reluctant mother to let her firstborn, in her words, "jump out of a perfectly good airplane." That time he had been strapped to the chest of a long haired granola-type guy he'd never met. Tandem, they called it. The sense of danger seemed muted since a) he felt like he was fastened into an oversized baby carrier, and b) he didn't figure Granola Dude was likely to bite it with him attached.

Despite the awkwardness of the situation, he and Dad loved it. He suspected Dad had paid the price, in one form or another, but he didn't seem to regret it. His first parachute descent was gradual, beneath a cruciform-style chute, which Granola Dude was able to control into a soft landing with a little upward kick into a running stop. It was easy.

He'd managed to convince himself that a post-ejection descent would be similar.

The second time beneath a parachute was in simulation for search and rescue training in Florida, learning how to manipulate the straps and release mechanisms, minimizing injury on impact, and not drowning in the case of a water landing. All quality information, gleaned from falling from a controlled environment, low to the ground, rather than being violently ejected into space after an explosion. The distinction made a difference.

The A-10 Warthog was intentionally and fabulously designed to take ground fire better than any fighter in production at the time. Some argue it retains the distinction. As a ground support fighter, it flies low and slow, circling its targets and unleashing a violent rain. Known for its ability to destroy armor, the Hog earned a reputation as a tank buster, and needed the ability to take a pounding from the ground.

The likelihood of encountering enemy anti-aircraft fire being great, the A-10 was capable of sustaining flight despite significant damage, including the ability to maintain flight after losing half a wing. It could not, however, sustain flight with the entire wing blown off, which precipitated the unfortunate pilot's third parachute jump.

This time, beneath the canopy of his ejection seat parachute, he spun wildly in swirling 20-knot winds. There were no lift characteristics, and no handles to guide with, just a dome-shaped piece of material packed into the ejection seat. Under it, he fell like an egg taped to a trash bag — something he and his brother once experimented with off the roof of their childhood home. He recalled the experiment perfectly, along with the tragic fate of a dozen cracked eggs that he prayed would not be replicated today.

He wondered if it wouldn't have been better to vaporize in mid-air rather than endure the expected pain he imagined the fast-approaching rocks were likely to inflict upon him.

His rate of descent was so fast, and the elevation of the terrain so high, he hardly would have had time to adjust to a proper landing anyway. All he could see was snow and rocks, and he suspected that the snow was just thinly covering more rocks. *This is going to suck*, he predicted.

Maybe the snow will cushion me, was his next thought, *like jumping into a snow bank*. He had done plenty of that growing up. *Snow doesn't hurt to fall in*, he tried to convince himself. *Okay, here it comes. Legs up, try to roll. Keep loose. No broken bones! No broken bones! I can handle this as long as I can walk. Here we go.*

He didn't roll, nor did he break anything, but he did hit hard, and with adrenaline pumping, he wouldn't feel the pain of impact as much on the first day as on the third. He went straight down; toes pointed down, he sank like a tent-stake, and was stuck up to the waist in deep snow, then a second later, was covered by straps, gear and the parachute, which flapped around wildly in the wind.

The blowing snow caused disorientation and he struggled to adjust to radically different surroundings. Minutes earlier he'd been strapped into a snug metal cockpit, impervious to the outer elements, secured by technology, engineering, and an inner sense of invincibility. Now, suddenly waist-deep in a snow bank, cold, wind, and shock assaulted him. He tried to push himself up and noticed his hands were shaking.

He stopped and looked around for a moment, felt

the snow beginning to seep through the thin flight suit's pants legs. Fear percolating, his next attempt was to dig his legs free. With a breaststroke motion, his cut a swath through the snow until he got some footing and was able to pull himself up and out.

His gloves were designed to withstand the cold environment of the cockpit, but they were breathable to facilitate the removal of moisture from sweaty palms, which was perfect gear for a pilot behind the controls, and entirely inadequate for digging in deep snow. The snow stuck to the thin fabric and the heat in his hands completely diminished in a few moments. He rubbed them together, stood up and looked around, trying to get an appraisal of his situation.

Training and common sense kicked in and he dropped into a low crouch, realizing that every enemy in the area had probably watched him descend. *Get down and out of sight, you moron.*

He looked around and saw large rocks off to his left, closer to the ridgeline. The snow was packed hard by months of wind on the saddle-like depression, which meant he could walk on top of it, but occasionally sank in as caked sections broke away underfoot.

He was leaving tracks everywhere, and stopped to look around. *What the hell do I do next?* His hand instinctively moved to the grip of his pistol in his chest holster as he scanned 360 degrees. The world was eerily quiet, and beautiful with the setting sun, the wind in his ears his only company. *For now*, he told himself.

He knelt down as soon as he reached the rocks and tried in vain to hide himself behind the largest one, pulling out his emergency survival radio and hoping to get through but keenly aware of the havoc that Afghan terrain plays on radio communication.

He knew he was being tracked by both sides, though

his beacon activated the second he ejected and only the good guys had a GPS fix on him. Voices on the other end of the radio confirmed what he already knew: a rescue mission was even now underway, but it would be close to an hour before evac could occur, slightly sooner for air cover to arrive.

He looked up and saw menacing clouds overhead. He knew what this kind of sky meant. *Batten down the hatches* is what he would have told his kids, and after taking care of outdoor chores, they would all look forward to a roaring woodstove, fresh soup and bread, warmth and laughter regardless of how much the wind blew against the windows. He loved winter storms at home, but not here.

In his present condition the weather was disheartening, and meant any rescue would simply be that much more complex, take longer, or be scrapped altogether, not because he didn't matter to the Air Force, to the contrary, but putting several air crews in jeopardy in order to rescue a single man was a calculation that any responsible commander would have to weigh.

He began to get scared. He looked around again. Visibility was poor and it was getting darker, meaning aerial surveillance wouldn't see him through clouds. Of course, neither would the enemy, he reasoned, and was comforted in the delusion that this may work out all right after all, the darker the better.

The next moment the wind -- stronger now -- bit his neck and he shivered hard. Dropping his chin to his chest, he flipped up the flight suit's collar, put on a brave face that nobody was around to see, and began to despair.

Ten legs ran as fast as the deep snow and uneven uphill terrain would allow. They didn't have the exact location, just a visual reference based on the direction of the parachute's descent as it fell below the ridge line.

Still, they were determined to reach him before anyone else did, and so kept moving at full speed. Having reconnoitered it for over a week, they knew the mountain well, and despite having made little contact with enemy troops, were well aware of their presence. A new urgency emerged when the wind picked up, mercifully to their backs.

Andy struggled to keep up with the SEALs as he had for the duration of the mission. Porter called a halt in order to get a visual, his bearings, and a breath. Were it not for increasingly poor visibility they would have a clear view of the path ahead; now they simply had to plow ahead using dead reckoning and memory. Andy, utilizing one of his radios, had managed to retrieve the coordinates of the pilot's beacon from the intelligence officers managing the rescue. A rescue mission was en route but couldn't be counted on to arrive in time. Andy and Porter looked at the digital map, and the pilot's location checked against their current position.

They began double-timing it in his direction. Another thing revealed by the radio communications: not only were they racing an unseen enemy, but a storm as well. They needed to find him before the storm set in, or he might disappear, enemy or no enemy. They ran, sank, got up again, tripped into deep snow, all the while scanning for enemies they knew were lurking; all heading to the same place, in haste.

The pilot used the parachute's strings to tie it into a tight ball and briefly attempted to dig into the snow to bury it when he looked up, paused, and changed his mind. There were a handful of things that needed to be done, but he spent several minutes spinning around in one place, trying to prioritize them, wasting critical minutes just trying to get it together.

How long it took was anyone's guess when suddenly the training kicked in, and he remembered a week of cold weather survival, evasion, resistance, and escape training, otherwise known as SERE.

Growing up in the woods had familiarized him with such topics prior to any kind of military training. He'd helped butcher caribou and moose by age 12 and was acquainted with subzero temperatures.

With no enemy in sight, he finally concluded the first order of business should be to minimize heat loss. His body temperature had dropped considerably in the past several minutes. The greatest danger was probably going to be exposure, and he needed to retain what warmth he still had.

His survival gear included a woodland camouflage jacket that he wished was white, vacuum-packed gloves and a wool hat, and a 15-degree sleeping bag. Unfortunately, the wind chill had it already below zero. This he knew because his nose hairs were freezing as they are wont to do around zero degrees.

He struggled to put on the wool gloves over his flight gloves, then the jacket, and once that was accomplished, considered whether or not to untie the parachute to use as shelter. *No*, he concluded after a short debate with himself, *too visible*. He would dig a snow shelter if it came to that, and he began to plot out a suitable location just in case. Up to this point he had not studied the terrain around him. *Oh, crap*, he thought.

He'd been prioritizing; focusing on step one, warmth, and step two, security. Now he recognized a serious problem pertaining to what could end up being steps nine and ten, extraction and rescue. It was a tactical problem and his pilot's mind began an assessment.

He was in a heavily sloped depression between two rocky peaks without much spacing between them. The ground was uneven, littered with large rocks that provided concealment, but coupled with deep snow all around that would make it impossible for a helicopter to land. Perhaps a small one could do it, but any rescue attempt would be conducted by a Chinook and this site was completely ill-suited for putting down the large aircraft. If they attempted to extract him from here they would have to hover and fast-rope in. Then they would have to hoist him and themselves up. The chopper pilot would have to correct for weight ratios both times when dropping the PJs off and then picking them all up again, in suboptimal visibility, high winds, and little room for fighters to cover the perimeter of the landing zone. It all added complexity to an already dangerous situation, even without the additional likelihood of enemy contact. *I've got to move to a better position.*

The canyon seemed to widen to the left, and he briefly radioed in his intention and its necessity. Gathering his bundle of gear, he moved in that direction. It was an exhausting twenty minutes of wading through snow, twice stopping to consider fashioning himself some snowshoes before rejecting the notion and moving on.

Finally settling into a much more open area, he collapsed with what he hoped was a very minor case of acute mountain sickness. The altitude was brutal, and with no supplemental oxygen his judgment was waning. He wondered how much longer it would be until he lost the ability to function altogether. Still, he'd improved his position.

Now, at least, the helicopter could land; he also wanted to keep moving as much as possible, denying the enemy a chance to catch up to him. This was a good spot, he figured. He would hunker down here, try to remain concealed, warm, alive. He found a place near a group of large rocks and spent a few minutes digging a cave-like depression in the snow with his flight helmet, crammed in the chute bundle, figuring if he had to, he'd get in the sleeping bag, slide into the cave and cover the hole with the chute. He only wished it were white, instead of drab olive green, to provide some camouflage.

The voice on the other end of the survival radio provided an update; fifteen minutes approximate, which, given the weather conditions of upper ranges in Afghanistan, could easily morph into fifteen hours.

Taking stock of his provisions, he frowned while examining the little pile in front of him: flares, a first aid kit, compass, survival tool, blanket, survival manual, light sticks, fishing kit – I guess I can floss at least, he thought – matches and flint, insect repellent, a candle, whistle, poncho, a saw, water filter, ten 4oz water packets, some food packets, and a few energy bars, not to mention his pistol.

The gun was as much a part of his flight gear as his helmet. Although no fighter pilot thinks anyone would ever have the audacity or skill to actually shoot him down, the possibility lurks in the back of his mind. So all fighter pilots carry a sidearm, though the standard issue 9mm Beretta held no appeal for this particular pilot. It was a decent gun with reasonable stopping power, but he'd grown up in woods that housed animals who could swallow 9mm rounds as appetizers before sinking their teeth into hapless hikers.

Figuring that if he were ever to hit the ground with bad guys and wild animals to contend with, he'd make sure he could kill anything that might pursue him, he carried a vintage Browning 1911. It was the other gift he'd received on that eighteenth birthday, the gift sanctioned by his mother, presented to him by his grandfather. Dad and Grandpa had taken him out to lunch, followed by a walk in the woods, coupled with some advice he never forgot.

His grandfather, a tender-hearted greybeard and a veteran, looked him for several seconds, measuring him with his eyes, then spoke.

He said, "Son, I hope you've learned by now how much we love and respect you. Now, you and I both know you're experienced enough, and your Daddy's raised you well enough to know the right choices over the wrong ones, but choosin' and doin' are two very different things. I want you to listen real hard now and look at me. Every decision you make for the rest of your life will result in a consequence. You need to ask yourself what that consequence will be before you act."

His grandfather pulled out the gun and held it in his open palms. "This weapon here will create a consequence every time you lift it. Be intentional, and accept the consequence. Do that with every decision you make from this point on."

It was a lesson he remembered vividly and reflected on often: in training, in his cockpit, while choosing his bride. Always a step ahead of his decisions, he was not used to having circumstances thrust upon him. Few were the number of times he'd been caught off guard.

One landed him here, the other landed him a wife.

He thought about Abby now, their two boys and their sixteen-month-old baby girl. *What if I don't make it out of here?* It was a possibility. Abby would be a widow, alone, his daughter never knowing a father. *No, that wasn't true.* Her grandpa and great-grandpa would be at every recital, every birthday. They would grill any boy who dared come to the house. They would take her for ice cream and buy her dresses, as would her uncles. She would be loved, provided for by men he loved, as would his wife. *They would lack for nothing. Nothing, that is, except me.*

Don't think about this. You're gonna get out of this. You're going to live. The helicopter will be here in twelve minutes or so. He thumbed the pistol, pulled the hat down tighter, then out of his peripheral vision, spotted something. A man, walking in his direction.

———

The helicopter bounced and jerked up and down in jarring spasms. The PJs thanked God that everyone aboard was a combat veteran, used to rough chopper rides. Green troops would be vomiting all over the place by now. Even so, most were pretty close to losing it. The turbulence mixed with anticipation for the mission made them antsy. Pumped up, ready to get on with it, they just wanted off the chopper as fast as possible.

The pilot announced they were ten minutes out. Checking weapons for the third or fourth time, everyone cinched straps, patted the outsides of pockets for the expected bulges from gear they wanted to have available at a moment's notice.

In the trail helicopter, Aiden and the other reserve PJs did the same. They would hold up and wait while the lead chopper went in and recovered the pilot. Aiden would only be involved if something happened to the lead chopper. All eight PJs in both aircraft went through mental calculations and were as ready as they ever would be, determined to rescue the pilot.

———

The SEALs were on firmer ground now. The snow was shallower and they were moving quickly, almost jogging while scanning, aiming, and moving in swift motions. Only about 300 meters left, uphill, but they should be coming around the bend in a few minutes, and expected to find the pilot right about there. It was almost dark and footing was tenuous so they had to watch for ice as well as enemies. They were almost there. Almost to him, and hopefully almost the hell off of this mountain.

———

The pilot froze, not sure whether to run or hide, and then instinct took over as he quickly dropped out of sight and made himself as small as possible. Slowly he pulled out the pistol and pressed it against his chest.

There were three of them. One with MANPAD (man-portable air-defense system) slung over the shoulder, two with AK-47s in hand, their heads scanning right and left, looking for him. They were still a little way off and hadn't seen him yet, but were heading in his direction, closer every second.

They didn't look anything like the coalition Afghan

soldiers he'd worked with. These were different, and they moved silently. He never would have heard them, and in the darkness he might have walked straight into them.

They might walk right by me, he wondered, *Maybe they'll miss me entirely. Hunch down and maybe blend in, hide till they're gone. Evade, survive, escape, right? Or something like that.* A week of in-field survival training flashing through his memory.

He sank down, and pleaded, *Please God let them pass me by.* The helicopter will be here any minute, and then — his thought process ground to a screeching halt as the implications of this crystalized. *Oh God, the chopper. A perfect target. These jihadists will hear it long before they see it.*

The future played out like a movie in his imagination. *It'll land right over there, he predicted, a mere stone's throw away, except they have a MANPAD They'll take careful aim, they'll let the chopper land up close, let them think there's no threat, a perfect ambush.*

He looked up, could hear fighters circling in an attempt to provide a perimeter of fire for the landing zone, but it was snowing now, visibility deteriorating by the minute, and the fighters' sophisticated visual displays were getting obscured. *If the bad guys couldn't see him, neither can the chopper, or the fighters*, the movie continued. *They'll hold fire unless they see a confirmed threat.*

But he could see them, right in front of him, and he would have to sit and watch as they put a rocket straight into the Chinooks rotor, or maybe right up the back ramp; a perfect takedown. *The chopper will flail around in a death spiral and smash into the ground, and then the guys with the AKs will rake anyone who might somehow manage to crawl out, mowing 'em down as they exit. There'll be PJs cut to pieces…maybe even…No!*

His hands got sweaty despite the cold, adrenaline

breeding anticipation and causing his heart to thump, his throat drying, resolution solidifying. He wasn't going to let them ambush the chopper. *Resistance.* He was going to take them out.

He raised the gun, took aim at... *Which one first?* The most important decision of his life hung in the air and he made some split-second calculations. *The MANPAD guy will be last, he'll need time to aim it. I'll pop him third. Two riflemen then — one looking this direction, the other looking away. I'll get the first guy and then hit the second when he turns around, startled by the shot.*

He had a plan.

He raised the pistol, aimed at target number one's chest. Doubt crept in. *You can't do this*, it lied to him. *This many targets, at this range, with this weapon, in this wind? Impossible. You've never been a great shot either. Your dad perhaps, your brother, but you?*

Stop it, he told himself, Concentrate. He went over everything he'd ever learned about shooting. *Take your time, take a breath, relax. You can do this. You have to do this.* His cupped his gloved left hand beneath his bare right one, his cold finger touching the trigger. Looking down the sight he tried to imagine a colored circular target, like he'd shot at a thousand times before, instead of the chest of the man in front of him. He willed himself not to look at the eyes, fearing a paralysis of morality. He'd dropped hundreds of bombs, and cut men to shreds with strafing runs his entire career, but somehow this was different. Still, he was going to kill this man, and for the same reason.

His finger stroked the trigger, but as he began to apply pressure lightening flashed — his world interrupted by searing pain and intense ringing in his right ear. His neck jolted and he saw stars intermingled with swirling snow as a rifle butt smashed repeatedly into the side of his head from behind.

His face was in the snow, everything was dark, pain and cold mixed with blood and heat. His brain tried to comprehend what was happening as he heard yelling; not English, something else. Kicks to his head, his chest, crotch, back, everywhere. Curling into a fetal position – a natural instinct of protection – he desperately moved his arm around searching for his gun. A foot smashed down on his hand and he recoiled further, moved his arms in close in a vain attempt to protect his head, completely on the defensive. No time to think as vicious blows rained down one after another.   The pain was dulled somewhat by the rapidity of it all and as he began to lose consciousness. He was being pummeled. They're going to kill me, he thought.

He saw   Abby's face; his beautiful wife smiling, laughing. He heard her voice, the last words she'd spoken to him just a few days ago over Skype, her signature signoff, repeated over multiple deployments throughout his long career.

"Come home in one piece mister," she always commanded him.

I'm so sorry Abby. The last words he would never hear. The pain of failure punctured his heart, the other pains gone. He'd failed everyone, those men on the ground earlier, his family, his country, the approaching rescue team. It was all over. Through the ringing in his head and the blackness that enveloped him he heard a faint, familiar sound in the far distance of a helicopter's rotor, and then nothing.

—

The Chinook pilot hovered, trying to gauge the

distance to the ground visually, but the snow was
blowing. Instruments told him he was almost low
enough so he scanned around through night vision but
couldn't make out anything. Suddenly he began hearing
enemy rounds ping the doors. The door gunners looked
for targets through the blowing snow but couldn't make
anything out, so they let out a burst and then waited.
The PJs were on the back ramp, poised to jump out as
soon as it lowered.

"We're taking fire," the pilot called over the
chopper's internal com.

Flight engineer Jason Holmes peered out over the
end of his minigun on the right side. He knew there
was a pilot out there, possibly ground troops as well,
he'd been told. Reluctant to fire at anything he couldn't
identify, he strained to see movement, but the snow was
intensifying, obscuring everything.

He searched for a target to expose itself, his gun
trained to the left when his peripheral vision caught
movement. Looking right he saw a streaking black blob
heading for his face. Flinching, he closed his eyes and
turned his head down to the right, and felt heat as the
thing whizzed past his face, exploding in the doorframe
less than two feet behind him. The shock threw him
across the chopper, metal ripping through his back,
shoulder, and neck. Blood sprayed from his multiple
wounds.

"Jason!" the other gunner shouted.

Two of the PJs got back on their feet from the jolt.
Regaining their bearings, they were immediately on top
of Jason, struggling to stop the bleeding as he flailed
and writhed. One held him down while the other
attempted to prioritize the multiple bleeding wounds
among bullets now penetrating the chopper hull.
Mercifully, the overwhelming pain caused Jason to pass

out.

The helicopter jerked violently, causing the other two PJs to stumble. Getting their rifles up again, they faced the Chinook's partially lowered back ramp, eager for it to open wide enough to jump down.

Before they could even see off the ramp, fire began pouring in. It was like opening the front door in a winter storm, only to be greeted by a blast of wind in your face. Bullets ricocheted around the interior as the ramp's gunner returned fire and the PJs dropped to their knees and did likewise.

Barely able to see past the ramp, they fired at unseen targets, fell backward, moving right and left to avoid the bullets, but there was no safe corner. A second rocket flew through the slit opening, hitting the inside of the chopper. The explosion sent the Chinook spinning and one of the PJs was thrown against the wall.

"Clint!" the other PJ, Brandon, shouted when he noticed his partner on the floor behind him.

Hot metal shards tore through Clint's left forearm, causing a single reflexive motion as the injured PJ let go of the gun, which now dangled impotent from his harness. Nerve cells communicated to his brain a searing pain that rocketed up his arm and through his spine.

"I'm hit," Clint replied through gritting teeth while grabbing his arm with his other hand; blood oozing through the fingers.

"How bad?" Brandon asked, sneaking quick glances at the wound while simultaneously trying to return fire. Clint just grimaced and let out a litany of expletives.

His arm's tore up. I'm going to have to deal with that, Brandon thought. *Clint's out.*

He looked back at the other PJs, whose hands were full working on the side door gunner. They were out too, the man was obviously critical, neither would be able to break away.

That leaves only me.

Brandon looked out into the snowy night. A pilot was out there, waiting. Maybe the enemy was on him by now, they were certainly close enough. The bullets kept whizzing by despite the ramp gunner unloading his minigun into the night. Brandon was mad, frustrated, desperate.

He'd trained for this so many times in exercises in the desert. A-10s had lit up the landing zone, keeping bad guys at bay, flares dropping all over the place. The Blackhawks would sweep in and two PJs would jump out, find the pilot on his knees waiting. They'd scoop him up, rush him back to the chopper, and be in the air in less than a minute.

That's how it's supposed to go. Every impulse told him to storm off the ramp, into the teeth of those bullets and find that pilot, killing all the bad guys he saw, but he couldn't even get off the damned helicopter.

That others may live. The words echoed like a choir in his ears. *This is what they meant.* He couldn't abandon that pilot, but there were critically injured men right here too, one bleeding profusely right next to him. *What do I do?* The answer revealed itself along with the resolution to carry it out as he remembered Aiden, Hector, and the rest on the trail helicopter, and feared that precious time was wasting away.

Get out of here and let them have it. Your crew is done, he admitted to himself as he radioed his decision to the pilot.

"Abort. Abort. Lift off. We've got two CAT-5s — abort. Let the trail chopper in."

The pilot was already fighting to maintain lift as alarms blared. He raised the controls and the Chinook attempted to limp away. The ramp gunner was still shooting as they increased altitude.

"Chalk 1, abort. Chalk 2, it's all yours."

Porter turned the bend just as the dark mass of the Chinook was lifting off, tilting to the left, and noticed a streak of smoke shoot out from the ground toward it. The missile flew past the evading fuselage and missed the massive helicopter. Porter's eyes followed the smoke trail back to its point of origin and he let loose on the spot with a series of short bursts, followed by a launched grenade.

Porter held his fire; two bodies lay in pieces before him. Suddenly it was eerily quiet. Daylight was gone, visibility completely deteriorated. Ray and Teddy knelt and pulled out their night vision, panned around but saw no sign of the pilot, or anyone else. As they spread out, something caught their attention, some sort of fabric, catching the wind and puffing up.

Swiftly they moved to the right with guns up. As they got closer they realized it was part of a parachute hemorrhaging from its bundle. Hope rekindled. The whistling wind gave way to the twin rotors of the other Chinook. Andy called to it, giving their position and asking the gunners to hold fire.

"LZ secure," he assured the skeptical aircrew. But as the door gunners looked out and saw figures on the ground with their backs toward the landing chopper, it was clear the ground dynamics had changed dramatically in the last few minutes. The bad guys had bugged out.

Porter stood, gun slung by his side, looking all round for any sign of movement. Ray turned toward him, gestured that they'd found something. Porter moved toward them, hopeful that they might just be able to take the bird landing behind him home.

———

Aiden was listening in as the command came in. "Chalk 2 inbound. LZ is hot."

That was it. The first chopper had been cut to shreds, the second was giving it another try. Their Chinook swooped in, did a 180-degree turn while the gunners searched in vain for targets. No incoming fire. Touchdown. The ramp lowered and Aiden leaped out, followed closely by the other three, scrambling in the darkness as they got their bearings, looking everywhere and quickly spotting a group of men, two standing, the others kneeling with guns pointed toward…nothing. This was not what Aiden expected to see.

Where the hell is he?

Aiden surveyed the scene. The only life he saw was a cluster of shadowy figures approximately thirty feet to his front, two standing in conversation with each other. Aiden strained to see if maybe the pilot was in between them. *Maybe he was safe already?* Aiden moved slowly. The man on the left was holding something, looking out into the distance, thinking.   Now the figure turned as if to finally take notice of the four approaching PJs. He'd seemed utterly indifferent toward them since they landed, but now he zeroed in on Aiden. Despair spread over Aiden when he realized that the figure was holding an empty flight helmet, its owner nowhere to be seen.

Porter turned, squared up with the younger PJ, then looked past him to the chopper before returning to a silent stare. The two men held a gaze for what seemed an eternity. Aiden stepped gingerly into the huddle and the stranger handed him the flight helmet; fear, uncertainty, and anger breeding in his heart. Failure.

You couldn't do a thing.

The pilot was gone.

Porter looked again at the Chinook's open ramp, the gateway to safety, the way off this mission, off this mountain. Reluctantly he made the call, the only call, and spoke into his mic. "Exit the area Chalk 2. Polaris in pursuit of Rapier. Moving out."

Aiden stared, confused. Porter leaned in close, hollered above the noise, "We know where they took him. We got to move now!" Without further explanation, Porter fell in line behind Andy, who motioned the direction he wanted the PJs to follow. The other three PJs briefly paused for affirmation from Aiden, who confirmed the order by following Porter.

The Chinook ascended into the dark night sky, swallowed up by snow and wind, leaving the collection of men to fend for themselves in the intensifying storm.

Gathering up what little survival gear the enemy had left in its haste, the PJs followed in single file. That others may live, each silently reminded himself.

Nine men snaked along the dark, desolate trail, high in the mountains of Afghanistan; four not knowing their destination or what to expect, five keenly aware of both, all hopeful of what they might find at its end.

4

DEBERG

10:30:00 EDT
United States Special Operations Command
MacDill Air Force Base, Florida

General DeBerg studied the wall of digital map displays. The three-star general was a former Delta operator, and currently in overall command of the unique units operating in various missions throughout Afghanistan, including Operation Trap Line, of which Polaris was part.

Operation Trap Line was his creation. Developed over the last year, it utilized intelligence gleaned, bribed, or lucked out of Afghan allies with the intention of hitting high-level Taliban in their winter quarters.

The mission was to perform reconnaissance over the remote-known enemy encampments and exploit targets of opportunity. The intel provided by human assets, satellite data, radio intercepts, and other means had revealed a handful of targets, mostly cave openings that could never be seen in a satellite image and were hardly noticeable even when standing twenty feet away. DeBerg had sifted through the options and selected four locations that looked the most promising.

Four teams were inserted onto four separate

mountains in the same general area, all within roughly equivalent support range, be it air-strikes, extraction, or quick reaction force, should things get exciting. Each team consisted of six men: four American special operators, an Air Force combat air controller, and an Afghan guide/interpreter. Three of the teams were US Navy SEALs— code named Arctic Cat, Polaris, and Ski-Doo. The fourth— code name Yamaha— consisted of US Army Delta Force operators.

Depending on circumstance, the four teams were authorized to engage targets, identify and/or eliminate or capture high-value individuals who might show themselves, or do what Arctic Cat had done yesterday: bomb the hell out of it. Having completed their mission, Arctic Cat – extracted five hours earlier – was drinking coffee, watching the drama unfold on the wall displays of their own base.

Ski-Doo had endured eight days looking at a deserted cave. With zero enemy activity and hours of uneventful night patrols in subzero temperatures, they'd been ordered to extract as well. That left Polaris and Yamaha in-field.

Both had cataloged enough enemy activity to warrant maintaining surveillance, but not enough to pull the trigger on an air strike. Several times each team had strikes called off at the last minute, command anxious for better opportunities that never materialized. Now the weather had become an insurmountable obstacle, and DeBerg decided to cut his losses and pull out his remaining two teams to reposition them on other target areas after the expected storm passed.

But as they were moving toward the extraction point, Polaris discovered their Afghan guide had walked them into an ambush. They had to call in air support to fight their way out, and the Air Force A-10 Warthog,

Rapier-One-Seven, had gone down.

SEAL Lt. Porter had ordered his team to switch directions to recover and protect the pilot. The Air Force's pararescue unit Raven had sent in its four PJs, and all of them were now on the ground doing God knew what, God knows where.

"Yamaha?" he asked his senior aide, eyes never leaving the maps.

"They're back. Probably in the mess hall or in bed already."

General DeBerg was not the kind of man who panicked, but he was frustrated. The order to extract the remaining teams had been given shortly after Arctic Cat's bombing — not because the op was failing; on the contrary, after eight days things were finally heating up. It was the weather. A major snowstorm threatened to cut off the notoriously sketchy communications, rendering air support impotent and eliminating any possibility of precision bombing.

Given that any snatch-and-grab opportunities would also be fruitless – they would have no way to take a captive in – there was literally no point in sustaining the mission, and rather than risk his men hunkering down to brave the elements, he had decided to bring them in for a few days and perhaps replace them with fresh teams. So DeBerg had pulled the plug. Two hours later Polaris had been ambushed.

Polaris had drawn the juiciest target. It was also the most difficult location, but according to the ultra-enthusiastic Afghan guide, was well worth the effort. DeBerg didn't know that the source of the guide's fervor was his desire to kill Americans in the most spectacular way possible, or he would have seen this as a warning sign. Next time he would. The cost of experience is often failure, and in war, that means flag-covered coffins.

DeBerg knew most of the men in Polaris and was acquainted with some of the PJs. All of the team leaders checked out, and Porter had a reputation that was enviable. Porter leading the ad hoc rescue that now consisted of nine men didn't scare DeBerg. He only feared what he couldn't control, and the weather in the mountains of Afghanistan was a killer more deadly than any man. The weather had gone angry; it was fully on top of Polaris and no choppers were going to be able to bring them out.

Everything just had to wait.

"Nothing from Polaris," the aide added, immediately wishing he could take back the obvious observation.

Polaris is full of veterans, all of these teams are. They can hole up for days, improvise, practically hibernate. Unless they come under fire there'll be no cause to worry. Of course if they do, we won't know. No coms. Always the damn coms in this country. Technology better than any in history, still we can't penetrate mountains and weather... Relax. It's always like this. Trust their training. Anything else to be done at this point? No. It's a waiting game now. Maybe get another cup of coffee.

The general thought about the pilot, glad that Porter was on his trail.

Another aide reported. "Sir, we have two F-16s on station circling above the weather. There's also a surveillance drone. The Chalk 2 Chinook is about to put down on the FARP at the base of the mountain." Anticipating DeBerg's next question, he added, "Chalk 1 is ten minutes out. Cat-5 casualty on the door gunner."

A Forward Air Refueling Point (FARP) was basically a portable gas station for helicopters, allowing allied helicopters to spend considerably more time flying while eliminating the inconvenience and hazards of aerial refueling. The Chalk 2 bird and its flight crew would wait it out on the ground, ready to leap up as soon as enough clouds lifted away.

DeBerg never took his eyes off the maps. "What's his status?"

"He took rocket shrapnel in the neck. A PJ on board was also hit but not critically. Surgeons at the NATO hospital are waiting for 'em." He added, "Two Hogs are inbound, same squadron as the missing pilot. It's gonna get crowded up there soon."

DeBerg ran the number in his mind from the ground up: *One pilot MIA, Polaris makes six, plus four PJs still on the ground, is ten.* He was responsible for putting them there and was responsible for bringing them all back. Then there were the chopper aircrews: one man critical, probably more injuries on that bird. *The second Chinook on the ground, waiting to go back in, four or five more makes approximately what? Nineteen?* Another Chinook was on its way to the FARP to replace the Chalk-One bird. Another crew, with fresh PJs – perhaps twenty-five men – not counting the fighters, aerial tankers, AWACS crews, and other support aircraft. He was responsible for every one of them, would take responsibility when the time came. Had done so many times in the past.

Still, he was confident.

This is war. Every one of those men were better trained and equipped than his generation had ever been. The concern he entertained for them didn't prevent taking calculated risks with their lives; risk is how wars are won. He was trusting Polaris to take their own risks.

They've been on that hill for ten days, he reasoned. *They know it better than any Americans on earth. Still, they can't remain there undetected forever. We already pressed our luck by staying this long. Too much risk.*

The calculations run in your favor for a while, but

the odds turn in time.

Can they find Rapier? Is he alive? Is it worth risking all those men to recover the body?

He knew what the men would say, but commanders are more sober. He turned to his aide more casually, not as a superior officer but in the tone of a friend who'd spent several decades bleeding in remote hills like this one. "Odds they can recover him?"

The slightly younger man thought for a moment, not looking at the general. "Thirty percent."

He's optimistic. DeBerg had figured it closer to ten percent.

Afghanistan played havoc with radio transmissions on clear days. This was a genuine blizzard. On a normal mission schedule Polaris would check in at prearranged way points or times. Now they were operating on contingency schedules, and Polaris was moving, quickly — where and how, nobody knew.

They won't check in until necessary. Will maintain radio silence unless the ground dynamics dictate otherwise. Be forced to hole up in the snowstorm, probably. If so, the pilot is as good as gone, may be already.

He knew the only thing that would call off the hunt were the elements, the enemy, or him. DeBerg looked at the clock. "How long till the wind lets up?"

"Estimate at least five hours," his aide answered.

Five hours. Okay Porter, you've got five hours to find him.

He turned, stared into the eyes of his aide. "The second it clears I want them extracted. If they don't have him by then, they won't."

His aide returned a firm nod and a look of understanding. "Yes, sir."

DeBerg turned back to the maps. "Keep the choppers at the FARP on alert. Get as much air over the LZs as possible, circle round the clock. I want a

Spectre up there too, ASAP," he ordered.

"Yes, sir," his aide replied, as he turned to relay the general's orders.

"Dan?"

"Yes, general?" he turned back. Their eyes met.

"When this goes down, I want all hell let loose on that mountain. Do you understand me? I want those men covered from every direction, full perimeter, a ring of damn fire around Polaris."

"Yes, sir."

Both knew it was already decided, but the general's words confirmed it officially. The general looked hard at the maps, remembered his combat days, and tried to imagine his operators' movements.

Let it go.

It was a lesson he'd learned through hard experience and heartbreak. Trust the troops to carry out their missions. He'd set the board, chosen the strategy, kept the time, but now it was up to them to execute. It was out of his hands.

Five hours. He checked the time in Afghanistan, 19:20:00. *It's dark now. You've got five hours to find him. I think I'll get some more of that coffee.* "Get me if anything changes."

"Yes, general."

5

THE RATS' NEST

On level footing – in a joint training mission, or in a multiple-branch competition, for example — PJs and the SEALs are closely matched, both highly composed of type-A personalities. But on this night, on this mountain, the PJs were getting their butts kicked.

It was mainly the altitude. The wind and snow were brutal, but the PJs were all Afghanistan veterans and had a long list of heroics on mountains. This was different.

Any ascension above 8,000 feet risks deadly pathological effects: headache, dizziness, flu-like symptoms similar to carbon monoxide poisoning, deteriorated alertness. In medical circles the term is

Acute Mountain Sickness, and it can affect even experienced mountaineers who routinely go above such heights. The risks increase the higher one goes, and High Altitude Pulmonary Edema — when the lungs fill with fluid and death can quickly follow — becomes an additional threat. The prevention for avoiding these ailments is prolonged acclimation, which is why mountaineers routinely spend several days at base camps before slowly trekking to higher elevations.

This is essentially what Polaris had done with their methodical hike to the original target, slowly ascending from a much lower insertion point. Having spent days in the thin air, the SEALs had no trouble walking or even running at this altitude. The PJs had no such luxury, having been whisked from their base in less than two hours' time. The four of them, Aiden, Dave, Hector, and Matt, were in as fine a shape as any professional athlete, yet the mountain was toying with them.

Aiden had an aching sense that the pilot was beyond their help, and he imagined what the enemy might be doing. It haunted him, drove him almost to the point of fury as he walked along, wanting to run. The demon of failure doesn't play fair; it accuses, washing away any rational examination of the circumstances, and leaves it's subject to stew and question what he or she might have done differently. There was nothing Aiden could have done to affect this outcome, but failure told him otherwise and made him want to hunch over and throw up — and not because of the altitude.

And yet, the man in from of him wasn't letting up. He didn't stop to rest. *That means something.* He just kept moving mile after mile like a machine that gave Aiden strength and encouragement. *These guys haven't abandoned hope, so there must still be a chance.*

Aiden hiked directly behind Porter. The SEALs
were evenly spaced among the PJs with Porter on point
and Ray taking up the rear. Gator and Teddy found
themselves in the middle of the PJs, all of whom could
barely hear over the wind, and could hardly see in the
blowing and deepening snow. Everyone worried they
might walk single file off a cliff. Many a man has frozen
to death walking in circles in a blinding blizzard,
sometimes around a warm cabin he simply couldn't see.
Porter knew the direction but was breaking trail in
deepening snow, and he still had to take into account
the lives of the men following behind. They pushed
ahead at a pace that would have killed most men and
severely winded seasoned climbers. One thing about the
human body— SEALs had it hammered home to them
every day of their careers— was that you can never tell
the limits of physical endurance. They were conditioned
to continue beyond the point of expectation, past
ability, forward to the mission's completion, or death,
sometimes both. SEALs have a motto, too: The Only
Easy Day Was Yesterday.

All nine pushed on.

Aiden squinted through his goggles, trying to make
out the shapes in the darkness, and saw Porter holding
up his hand. He signaled for the line to hold its position
and Porter went back to speak with Andy near the rear
of the column. A few minutes' conference and Porter
again pushed past him, retaking the lead and veering
sharply left. Frustration seethed within Aiden as he
realized they'd been moving in the wrong direction,
quickly replaced by fear as he wondered how far off
course they were and how much time had been wasted.

*Do they even know where we are? Is he as good as dead
already?*

He put the pointless questions aside as quickly as

they came. There were no options but to plow ahead, and no point in thinking about things he couldn't control. Either they were going to find him and rescue him, or fail. Either he was already dead and they would find his body, or they would fail and have to live with the knowledge that they tried. In any case, they had to keep going to see which way it would play out. So he focused on his breathing, footing, and keeping pace with the guys ahead of him. Whenever they got where they were going, he intended to be there with the strength to fight.

Still, he wondered. *Are we looking for a cave, a bunker, a camp? Will we have to go in with guns blazing? Are we going to an observation point? Searching for friendlies, or intel?*

There had been no time to ask questions before they set out, but the questions kept popping nonstop in his head.

Just keep moving. Deal with it when we get there.

Just as he was mustering up the will to push himself another hour, Porter again abruptly held up a hand and stopped. He pivoted left, went forward another twenty feet or so, and then disappeared. Aiden was stunned and blinked, wondering if he was hallucinating or if Porter had just fallen off a cliff. As his eyes adjusted to the new terrain he realized that Porter had slipped behind a small cluster of rocks. Porter's frame emerged again and motioned at them to move forward. Aiden looked around as he entered the alcove and was grateful for the protection against the wind it afforded.

Is this it?

The little grouping was a haven from the wind but the snow continued to fall in the dark. The rest of the procession caught up quickly and squeezed into the rocks.

"End of the line. Hold up," Porter said. Aiden

watched the officer look around, searching for his team, saw Porter point two fingers at a slender black man and a huge white guy, followed by a hand motion that ordered them to begin surveillance. The duo walked past Aiden, disappearing around the dark corner.

"We're here." Porter looked at the PJs, and scoffed under his breath, "Home sweet home."

Almost everyone took a knee, coughing, shaking their heads. Only Aiden and another of the SEALs remained standing.

If a coach had ever ordered Aiden to take a knee on the hockey rink, or basketball court, he'd obeyed immediately, but if it was only a suggestion, Aiden always remained standing. He never felt kneeling was appropriate outside of church. Perhaps it was pride, though he wasn't an overly prideful person; he felt kneeling was synonymous with submission, giving in, or reverence. At the very least it signaled the need to rest, and he always wanted to convince himself that he could go a little longer. He was always the first person back to drill, the first one back on the line, and the last one to leave the ice, the gym, or the field. He was always the last kid in the door, not because his mom had to yell at him, but because he was the one who would pick up the mess that the other kids left outside. It was a trait that all of his coaches, instructors, and commanders noticed immediately, and it had influenced his progression within the ranks.

———

Porter noticed him standing and had the same impression as so many others. As Porter began to turn away, Aiden interrupted, pointing in the direction the two men had just moved.

"Where are they going?" he asked.

Porter answered while mentally sizing him up. "They'll be back. Going to have a look."

With that, Porter took a swig of water from his canteen and seemed to be thinking. Everyone else just waited. After a few minutes Porter rubbed a hand over his eyes and noticed Aiden poised, looking anxious.

———

On a ridge less than ten feet away, Ray delicately pulled out his sniper rifle and peered through the night vision scope. Teddy lay next to him, taking in the same scene through the spotting scope. Both strained to get clarity through the falling snow. Sudden gusts threw off their concentration but they'd lain in this very position so many times over the previous week that the ice beneath the snow had molded to their contours. There was something comfortable about that. They'd spent hours, days, here, watching a narrow cave entrance below, several hundred meters away from them. Over that period of time Ray had drawn a bead on scores of enemy sentries but there'd never been more than one or two at a time.

What they saw on this night was much more interesting. The increase in activity was evident at first glance — typically the enemy they'd seen had been at ease, casually standing around, sometimes smoking.

The situation had changed dramatically.

This time their targets — four of them— were standing erect and visibly edgy with weapons poised and fingers on triggers. Two kept stealing glances into the cave, occasionally darting inside only to be shooed back out by a fifth and much angrier, fatter, sweaty man they'd never seen before. Two of the five were familiar faces. Ray had previously snapped pictures of every face he'd seen for cataloging, and didn't recall ever having seen any of the other three. All five were looking around nervously, expecting something any moment. The wind, coming up against the sentries' left side, was causing the outside four to turn their heads slightly right, only glancing left when the wind abated. None had goggles, nor any visible flashlights.

Ray smiled. The extra activity was exactly what the SEALs had hoped to see, indicating there was something worth protecting inside the cave. The enemy was tasking four men to stand out in a windy snowstorm at night protecting…what? Ray and Teddy watched for a few more minutes and then slunk backwards.

Teddy reported back, "We'll need to approach from the right. Wait for a good gust of wind and they'll be looking the other way when we turn the corner and move fast. Can't tell what'll be in there when we get inside though, never could see much inside but it's definitely buzzing tonight."

Porter nodded. There was a brief moment of silence as they all pondered what the next step would be. He had a decision to make.

Polaris had already planned this mission, had run through all the variables a hundred times in their heads and in the dirt of their hide. In the last few hours the tactical situation had changed with several contingencies to factor in. It was still a snatch and grab, but with the added complexity that the person they were hoping to snatch might be badly injured, and getting him out quickly without further injuring him might be impossible. That likely wouldn't have been a large calculation if it were a bad guy, but now it mattered.

Fortunately it was night, an inestimable advantage. On the other hand there were now twice as many targets to eliminate on the exterior, and still unknown numbers inside, but at the very least as many as were outside, and probably more. Add in the enemy's new alert status, and it had become about as dicey as it gets.

Porter decided he needed more shooters.

He looked at the PJs. Porter knew PJs were elite; he'd worked with plenty of them before but he also knew that probably none of them had ever undertaken this kind of assault before. PJs were trained to swing swiftly into hot zones to treat Americans and transport them out before the dust settled. This was decidedly different.

Most men in training fail at room clearing as miserably as Porter had, with instructors up in the catwalks above the recruits, drilling them over and over till they learned the deadly lessons and eventually mastered the art. Porter hoped the PJs had some basic training with it, but he'd had enough run-ins with less than adequate support troops to take nothing for granted. But, war is war, and you play the hand you're dealt. He resisted the urge to ask if they'd ever done anything like this before; he knew they hadn't so it didn't matter. And he didn't want to plant a seed of doubt in their heads. They were going to do it, whether they felt prepared or not.

Porter looked at Aiden. "One of your guys will stay here and cover my sniper's six with Andy. The rest of you will follow us in and clear the cave."

Aiden looked him straight in the eye without the slightest reaction.

Porter continued, "We'll go in single file and clear away the guards as we go. Y'all follow close behind and watch the flanks and shadows in case we miss any. Hit anything that's not our pilot with three in the chest and keep moving unless we tell you to stop."

He looked around at each of the PJs as he spoke. "Close enough to put a hand on the shoulder of the guy in front of you, okay?"

Aiden nodded. The other PJs seemed equally dialed in and determined, and although Porter had expected some nervous looks, he got none. These guys were steel. Porter was inwardly relieved.

"We're going to approach slow, and very, very quietly. Slow and smooth, and watch your footing. Our rifles are suppressed, so don't fire yours unless you have to. Keep it tight. The last man in the line needs to hold up just inside the opening, turn around, and cover our six."

Porter was drawn again to look at Aiden, confident he understood completely.

"Matt, that's you," Aiden said, pointing him out for Porter.

Porter continued, "Okay, Matt, take up the rear. Ray will be covering from up here."

"Affirmative," said Matt.

Aiden looked at his other three PJs, and pointed at Dave. "You stay here."

Dave was the youngest and least experienced of Aiden's PJs. Aiden hadn't worked or trained with him much, and so he didn't know how much he could rely on him.

Porter concluded, "Any questions?"

For a few seconds they looked around, then Aiden asked, "Do you know the layout inside?"

"Nope," Porter answered abruptly. "We've never been inside. Been in these sorts of caves before though, and you never know what to expect. Some are caveman ancient, others are five-star extravagant. There's just no tellin', so stay close and don't touch anything until we call it clear." Then he added as an afterthought, "Don't treat the pilot, or even go near him until you hear us call it clear. Alright?"

Everyone nodded in agreement. They knew the enemy well enough to know that a body strapped with explosives to fry compassionate Americans was a disgusting tactic that had claimed lives and limbs in the past. The PJs had treated plenty.

"Alright. Gator, take the point. Teddy, go behind me, and you," he pointed at Aiden, "bring in your guys behind him. Remember, stay close behind Teddy."

Aiden nodded again.

Everyone dropped their extraneous gear and checked their weapons. A few minutes later they were ready and got in line as Porter had directed.

Five minutes later the three SEALs were moving down a narrow trail followed closely by the three PJs. The trail was covered in ankle-deep snow but Gator had memorized the approach over the past several days and could have felt his way along blindfolded, which, given the current conditions, was practically the same thing. Attention to detail made the difference between successful missions and dead sailors, something his instructors had beaten into his head over and over. Gator had carefully planned this assault from two angles in order to give them options when the time came, and now that attention to detail was paying off.

The speed of their descent in the dark, blowing snow told the PJs that the SEALs were intimately familiar with the ground, and gave them hope that the pilot might actually be there.

Polaris had patrolled this area every night since landing on the mountain after trying and rejecting three other approaches. They moved fast; Gator knew every step by number, where the trail rose, when the entrance would come into view, and how many seconds it would take to get into position. Of course, the deep snow was going to throw that out of whack, but Gator had also planned for that.

Gator crept forward, placing his feet down as lightly as possible to minimize the crunching sound of boots on snow, a sound blessedly masked tonight by the howling wind. The SEALs moved in perfect symmetry, evenly spaced, close enough to touch the man in front but far enough back so as to not stumble into him if he suddenly stopped. Initially Aiden had worried about keeping up, but as soon as they moved down the hill and leveled out, the line crept to a snail's pace.

Aiden stole a brief glance over his shoulder to verify Matt and Hector were keeping up; both were right behind, perfectly in step, confident, weapons ready. Returning his gaze forward, Aiden realized Teddy was several steps ahead. He considered moving faster, but mindful of making too much noise he simply kept moving, slow and smooth, hoping Teddy would ease up so he could catch up. Simultaneously anxious, nervous, and eager, Aiden controlled his fear, sparking positive aggression and sharpening his focus. He hadn't trained for this exact scenario but he knew the fundamentals inside out. The PJs trained with their weapons just like every other Special Forces operator and were fully proficient.

Aiden wasn't scared of what he was about to do, only the outcome. He feared for the fate of the pilot. They were still after him, had done everything possible up to this point to recover him. He was desperate to get into that cave. He wanted to run in with guns blazing and find him, protect him, and get him the hell out of there. The slow methodical movement was infuriatingly proper.

Gator pulled up abruptly. They were at the jumping off point. The next step would take him around the corner, and thirty feet after that to the right was the cave entrance. He keyed his mic. "Polaris three in position."

—

Ray couldn't see them yet through his sniper scope but knew they would momentarily pop into view. Andy, next to him with the spotting scope, was scanning for additional movement. Ray planned on taking out the guards from his position, clearing the way for the assault team to enter. It wasn't a long shot and he routinely hit targets from greater distances. The problem was the cold reliability of physics — under these wind conditions he doubted he could put a bullet on target, much less center mass, and now there were four sentries.

Under perfect conditions Ray would take out more than two in quick succession. He knew that as soon as he popped bad guy number one the body would fall, probably make some noise, and catch bad guy number two's attention, making the target move, which would alter Ray's shot and increase the time to home in on number two. With four targets to eliminate, it was out of the question. Instead, the team on the ground would have to take them out one by one, and the guys up above would provide cover as needed and reinforcements if necessary. In this scenario, Ray had his sights trained on the man to the extreme left, the one Gator would reach last, the one most likely to have time to respond to an assault force.

All of the SEALs had qualified in close-quarters room clearing. Their first taste had been in the latter stages of BUD/S training, where everyone fails. The variables are simply too numerous to fully prepare for. After several attempts most candidates become proficient, and none graduate without doing so. But from the start everyone knew Gator was different — in BUD/S, he had put up perfect scores. Later on, when Gator entered the door of the live-fire house, he could feel the instructors' gaze from their perches in the rafters, almost wishing for his failure but also rooting for his perfection while they evaluated the entrance, speed, rate of fire, and every other factor. Terrified of screwing up yet confident in his approach, he methodically moved from room to room, aware that failure might result in being bumped down to a different rotation, or dismissed outright and relegated to a different unit. But this was where he longed to be. When he'd finished, he held his breath, anxiously awaiting the instructors' critique. The resulting thumbs-up for passage was overshadowed by the instructors' head-shaking amazement at the perfection of his execution. Gator had impressed them, and would continue to do so at every stage of his SEAL career.

Porter trusted him completely and he followed him now.

Gator took a deep breath and listened for the go signal from Ray, who would say "execute" as soon as the nearest guard turned to look the opposite direction. The wind was at Gator's back and the gusts wrapped icy snow around him, stinging his cheeks and momentarily obscuring his goggles. None of the enemy had goggles, nor glasses, though all had thick beards, jackets, and head coverings that left only their eyes exposed.

Ray watched them turning, looking, turning back again with guns ready. If the timing was off, Gator would walk straight into the muzzle of a waiting AK-47. Ray hesitated. Another large gust blew in, all four guards quickly turned to their right. Ray made the call.

"Execute."

In a flash Gator turned the corner and saw the back of a man moving away, brightly illuminated in his night vision. Gator rushed forward, aimed at the center of the back, pulled the trigger twice. *One down.* The shape fell forward revealing another man's back three meters ahead. Gator kept his feet moving steadily forward, stepping around the body as he put two more into the next shape, then panned left, then quickly to the right as he stepped over the body and kept moving forward. Porter behind him put another round in the first body as he too passed over it, and repeated with the second. In less than four seconds he was at the right edge of the cave entrance.

Gator trained his sight on the next guard on the opposite side of the entrance. The man turned to face Gator, who noticed the look of shock in his eyes and knew the man's brain was computing what was happening. Gator's kneeling added an extra variable for that brain to process and caused his eyes to lower. Porter seeing Gator kneel in front of him spotted the enemy looking down and put a bullet in his forehead at the same time Gator put one in his chest. *Three down.*

The last enemy standing heard his companion's body hit the ground and turned, but as he did, the wind made his eyes shut instinctively. By the time he saw the man on the ground it was too late to aim his rifle. He never got it up.

Ray's shot dropped guard number four, hitting the man in the armpit as he attempted to raise his weapon. Ray scanned to the left for more targets and briefly paused on each of the fallen guards, then checked their flanks on either end, finding no movement. Finally he settled his cross-hairs on the void of the cave opening.

Gator kept his kneeling posture and watched the fourth man go down. He clearly saw the man was dead and didn't need to confirm it with another shot. There was no time to lose. He quickly peered around the rock into the cave entrance.

Porter moved up close behind Gator and placed a gentle hand on his shoulder, a signal to let him know he was supported from the rear and that they were ready to proceed at Gator's lead. Gator's night vision illuminated everything in the dark and he could clearly see there was nobody in the immediate entrance, but farther in was a path leading to the right and some light was seeping from it. Gator keyed his mic. "Moving."

Gator turned to his left, the rifle leading his steps. He kept looking right as Porter entered directly behind him and looked to the left, toward the dark corner Gator couldn't see. Aiden followed Porter's motions, directly behind him. As the three of them entered and moved farther into the opening, Teddy followed, double-checking every shadowy crevice he saw. Hector was right behind Teddy, mirroring him.

Matt watched them disappear into the darkness and turned around to cover their rear. He suddenly felt very alone. With a cold darkness behind him, an even colder darkness in front of him, and nobody to be seen, he might as well have been on the moon. Yet the knowledge that a sniper was covering him from above was a measure of comfort. He turned his head slightly to see if he could hear shots, but heard only silence.

Gator crept forward in the darkness, following the only path into the depths. He had experienced two similar missions before and expected to see movement any second. He held up when he was close enough to move into the light, waiting for Porter; he again felt a gentle squeeze on his shoulder and knew Porter was ready. He moved forward, faster now around the corner to his left. As he turned he saw two men standing and talking, and another sitting on the floor, eating. The man on the floor was looking straight at Gator as he turned the corner and scrambled for his rifle, bread falling out of his hands and mouth. Gator fired three rounds at him, hitting him in the ribs and throat. Porter fired at the man standing on the left, sending him flying backwards on top of the eater.

The last man standing faced Aiden and turned to grab a rifle leaning against the wall but Aiden shot him once in the side and he fell forward in a lump, face first against the sharp rocks that made up the wall. The sound from Aiden's rifle rang in everyone's ears and the SEALs moved faster, knowing that there was now no possible element of surprise. They still didn't know how far back this cave went and how many more men they might find in it.

As Gator moved past the man on the ground, he saw another light around another corner and moved to it. He looked inside, saw a figure from behind, scrambling, searching for his weapon. The figure had been kneeling on top of a sleeping bag, and appeared to be going through a pile of articles. Gator fired one bullet in the rib cage, and another in the neck as he fell forward. Gator aimed his rifle at another man on the ground, but this one had a very different look — his face was bloody and had clearly been beat to hell. He appeared to be unconscious. He was wearing a flight suit.

Gator turned back to the man he had just killed, put two more bullets into his back just to be sure, and then turned around, looked at Porter, then at Aiden.

"Clear!"

Porter, with a two finger swipe through the air, beckoned Aiden to tend to the man. Aiden looked at him, and fear mixed with relief flooded over him in the fraction of the second it took for his training to take over. He quickly knelt beside him checking for vitals; the pilot was alive but unconscious. He was covered with blood, and his face, especially his left eye, was swollen and bruised. Aiden took his pulse, then pulled out his flashlight and shined it across his eyes, pulling his eyelids up and getting a small response. He wanted to start pumping fluids into him right away and get going on first aid. He was just about to pull open his pouch with IV and fluids when he stopped and remembered where he was — not in the safe confines of a medically equipped Blackhawk, but in the depths of a dark, dank cave, recently occupied by America's worst enemies.

The man was stable and needed out of there. He paused and wondered what chance the pilot would have if they couldn't properly treat him soon. Aiden had no idea of the extent of his injuries. He could have a broken neck, or spinal damage, internal bleeding, or any number of other issues. Moving him a few feet could be fatal. He was probably already in shock and the temperature or blood loss alone could kill him.

Hector was on the man's other side making the same medical calculations. They looked at each other, Hector waiting for Aiden's reaction, wanting him to make the call. Aiden looked at Gator, who was going over the dead man's body searching for…something. Aiden saw Gator pull a pistol out from behind the dead man's shoulder. The SEAL looked at it momentarily and then whistled. Aiden looked up and saw Gator working the slide on the aged Browning 1911. Aiden recognized the pistol, and the worn marks on the original handle. It would have made a nice trophy of war for these creeps had they not paid for it with their lives.

Gator moved over to the pilot and looked over Aiden's shoulder. "Nice gun. I'm guessing it's his," and then handed it over to Porter, who had just come up behind him. Hector glanced up, then back at his patient. Porter took the gun and put it into a pouch inside his vest and stared for a second at the pilot, then at Aiden. Aiden's eyes locked on Porter, who said, "We need to move, now." Then he added, "What can we do to help you?"

Hector, looking over the pilot, asked, "Stretcher?"

The cave had three chambers that were rather large, but in order to get to them they had almost squeezed through two very narrow turns. There was no way they could get a seven-foot stretcher around the bends. In fact, there was no possible way to move him out of the cave without jostling him intensely. The irony was, the movement of him to safety might kill him, but that was usually the case. This was part of the job, the part that many PJs would have enjoyed for the challenge except for the deadly considerations. There were problems to be solved and challenges to overcome in every mission. That was the reward, the rush, when successful. When the problems overtook them, and results were fatal, well…that is why they each carried a carefully folded American flag, and why some of them had nightmares.

Aiden shook his head, "Not enough room." He

paused "We'll walk him out. Let's get him up."

Knowing the extent of his injuries would require an exam at the very least, plus x-rays, monitors, luxuries they didn't have, not yet anyway. Nor did he have time to immobilize him and find out. They needed to get out of this cave. Aiden would have to risk it. Hector lifted him up to a standing position and Aiden grabbed the jacket and the hat off of the man Gator had just shot. Though it was warm in the cave, it was below freezing outside and the pilot would surely freeze to death without it. They struggled to get it on him and eventually got him to a standing position with Aiden and Hector each under one of his armpits while the pilot's awakening legs struggled to find strength. Thankfully, both PJs were taller than the pilot they were carrying.

"Lieutenant, grab that sleeping bag and wrap it around him."

The SEAL was glad to help with something. Porter looked and saw a US issue emergency sleeping bag in the corner, another trophy of war for the pilot's abductors. They probably fought over them, and this guy had won the prizes, short-lived though they were. Now Porter took the sleeping bag, partially wrapped it around the pilot's shoulders, tucked it under Aiden's and Hector's arms and pulled it around his torso. Once they could lay him down again Aiden would make sure he was tucked tight into the bag. For now it would be good insulation for the pilot's core when they got outside.

Aiden and Hector carried him past Teddy, who was tearing apart the laptop computer they'd found on the table. He expertly removed the hard drive and tucked it away in one of his pouches. He also searched the CD-ROM drives for any discs and went through the pockets and satchels of each of the dead enemies.

Gator went over them again after the PJs moved past, and all three SEALs took one last look around the cave they had spent so many hours preparing to exploit or destroy. Porter looked at them both and asked, "Got it?" He got nods from Teddy and Gator as they rose up and proceeded to follow the PJs out.

Matt had been waiting anxiously at the cave entrance, eyes darting left and right, every windswept snowflake drawing his aim. It felt like forever until he finally heard Aiden's voice call to him from behind. "Behind you. We clear?" Matt turned and looked at Aiden and Hector, then back toward the entrance again.

"We're clear. You guys ready to move out?" he asked.
The PJs moved over enough to let Teddy and Gator squeeze past them, and without stopping they moved swiftly out into the night.

Matt was right behind him, thankful to have someone in front of him again. Aiden and Hector moved past with their patient between them. As they exited, Gator held up and fell into position behind them again. Porter was the last man to exit the cave into the cold wind, Teddy leading the procession back up toward the ridge.

As Porter walked out he looked up toward Ray, and keyed his mic. "Polaris one. Rapier-One-Seven recovered."

Part II

Vince Guerra

6

AA0x4

22:00:00
Afghanistan

There was a stirring in the dark place. He smelled something foul. It was musty and reeked of body odor and mold. He tried to open his eyes but pain shot through his face. He relaxed his brow and tried to listen, but didn't hear anything. He took in a breath and wanted to vomit.

He was cold. He tried to comprehend his surroundings, faintly remembered taking aim at figures in the snowy twilight before everything went wrong. He remembered the kicks and punches until everything faded away. Now he was alone and didn't know what to make of it. He was certainly alive. The searing pain confirmed that. Two good things about pain he'd heard growing up: it tells you you're still alive, and it prevents you from doing further damage.

Where am I? He tried to move and was instantly aware of a splitting pain in his head, back, ribs, and eye. Stars filled his vision and he curled up, panting for air.

He heard gunshots. Still unable to open his eyes, he wondered if he'd just been executed, but no, there were other sounds. He was on the edge of a dream. He heard voices, felt someone pulling open his eyelids, bright light shining — but just like in some dreams, he could not move his arms or legs, or speak. He remembered fragments of cloudy, sporadic details, like pieces broken from the main puzzle.

He heard voices; English-speaking voices, and someone tugging at his leg. He felt someone picking him up and pain racked him from head to toe. He felt his feet being put onto the ground and something in him instinctively tried to walk. He was amazed his feet and legs didn't hurt. Finally something was working and it gave him a degree of clarity, but still he was floating.

No, not floating. Someone is carrying me.

His breathing was shallow, no moisture in his throat, jabs of pain scattered throughout his body. The voices were talking to each other but he didn't hear them.

Suddenly he was aware. He knew what was happening to him. He tried to look at the men carrying him with his good eye straining to the right. All he could see was the man's chest. He tried to speak again but they were moving quickly, and he was having a hard enough time breathing. Then he felt the blast of cold.

The relative quiet was shattered by howling wind. It was the most unbelievable cold he had ever experienced. The wind stung his face and his bloody eye with the force of a shotgun. He almost passed out again except his legs suddenly sunk into deep snow, and he instinctively stepped up and out of it. The men carrying him were stumbling and his body's natural inclination toward self-preservation kicked in. He was walking now, if for no other reason than to get somewhere out of the cold. With Samson-like effort he raised his voice and shouted, "Where are we going?" but nobody answered. The wind was howling in his ears and he wondered if they were ignoring him. Then he doubted he had actually made any sound. He struggled through the pain, using legs that did not want to move, his body spent, but the figures kept moving him as he prayed he would soon be pulled out of the cold wind and into a helicopter.

They're taking me to a helicopter. I don't hear one but it can't be much farther. This will all be over soon. Thank God.

No noises but the wind, and the ruffling of the fabric around him. An eternity later he stopped. He tried to speak but was out of breath, his lungs on fire. He felt a tremendous weight on his chest like being underwater. The voices, he could understand. He was being laid down; felt a cold wind surround him. His body temperature dropped another several degrees as the sleeping bag was pulled from his back and chest. Someone was easing his legs into the sleeping bag.

Yes, thank you, he thought.

His arms and legs were zipped up, only his face exposed. Someone was leaning over him. He opened his eyes and saw a dark figure, shining a flashlight. He heard a voice that sounded sort of familiar. English. American. Southern?

"Sir. Can you hear me, sir?" Hector asked
"Yes."
"What is your name, sir?"

It was the first step in determining the extent of his injuries. There would be a sequence of four questions

— name, location, time, and the event that caused this meeting — each of which would give the PJ a good assessment of the patient's level of consciousness. He was awake (A), and he was alert (A), oriented (O), and if he could answer all four questions correctly, he would be designated AAOx4, as alert, awake, and oriented times four — or times three, two, or one, if he were completely disoriented.

The pilot understood this was probably what was happening, but the officer in him had another set of principles working. He was inherently cocky, didn't know who this guy was, and had regained enough of himself to muster up his own question.

"Who's asking?" he replied.

Hector was taken slightly aback, surprised that the patient was more alert than he'd expected. Hector sat up a little straighter and replied, "Unites States Air Force pararescueman Hector J. Galindo, sir. What is your name, sir?"

The pilot smiled, relieved to be speaking with an Air Force PJ.

"Captain Josiah McCoy, U.S. Air Force."

"Where are you?" Hector asked him, getting back to business.

"Afghanistan, God help me." Humor, good. AAOx2, Hector noted mentally with a smile of his own.

"What day is it?" Hector asked. He could have asked what time it was, but on the battlefield, and at night, the question was impossible to ascertain. Hector himself didn't even know what time it was.

Josiah answered, "It was Wednesday when I got shot down. They took me the same day. I have no clue what day it is now. You tell me."

Hector was satisfied. The patient remembered getting shot down, the circumstance that brought him here, and his predicament. He was AAOx4. Hector still had one more question though. "Thank you, sir. I need to ask you this, who won the last time you and your brother played chess?"

Josiah gaped. The answer was Aiden.

He thought for a moment. Yes, the last time he and Aiden were together was between overlapping deployments at Christmas, a year and a half ago. They drank coffee and played games at their parents' house until 3:00 am Christmas Eve, country music playing on the radio. They had relished that night, not wanting to talk about war or the military. That Christmas, all they wanted was to forget everything in Afghanistan and relive the carefree days of growing up, playing games. They had spent so much time killing bad guys with sticks in their woods, and so much time dealing with real bad guys over the past few years, that the mere thought of it exhausted them. They wanted escape, and so they stayed up, not wanting the night to end, and played chess. Aiden beat him with six pieces left on the board between them.

Why is this guy asking me about Aiden? Suddenly it came to him — Aiden was a PJ. This guy was from Aiden's unit.

"He did," Josiah answered, "but I smoked him at Madden." Josiah let out a mild chuckle that caused a fit of painful coughing.

Josiah raised his head to look around while trying to ignore the pain of his swollen eye. He had to move his head and shoulders in order to compensate for his lost vision.

There.

Josiah saw the profile of a soldier kneeling, with his weapon up, slowly sweeping for threats. He couldn't see the eyes behind the goggles, but he could tell it was his brother.

Hector pulled Josiah's hand out of the sleeping bag and put in an IV, then put a thick mitten over his hand and tucked it in as snug as possible. Hector hung the IV from a portable stand and began feeling around under Josiah's clothes for additional injuries. Josiah lay back, let him do his exam, and thought about his brother, over there protecting him.

It dawned on Josiah that all of these guys were likely here because of him. How many resources had gone into finding him? Josiah made mental calculations, including ground assault troops, chopper crews, support aircraft, drone monitors, and a hundred other things that went into rescue operations for downed pilots. He wondered if there was news stateside about it.

Does Abby know? Has she told the kids that daddy was shot down? That Aiden was looking for me? He dismissed the thought. *Of course she wouldn't tell them anything like that, but they might suspect something...how long has it been?*

Josiah had just formed the question in his head and was about to ask Hector when he saw Aiden approaching. He tried and failed to sit up to meet him, and Aiden knelt down on his left.

"You know Abby's gonna to be pissed, right?"

Aiden loved his sister-in-law's sass. He'd know her since they were kids. He knew she always said the same thing to Josey right before she kissed him goodbye on deployment night: "Keep it in the sky, you stud." And Josiah always promised her he would. Now he had to go back and eat his words. And though he had no doubt she would cry hot tears over his return, she was equally likely to slap him as soon as the kids were out of sight for making her worry. She would also probably tease him about it for the rest of his life. Josey began to ache, this time out of a maddening need to hold his wife.

"Don't lie to me, how hurt are you?" Aiden asked. His brother never admitted injury; not to his parents, not to his wife, not to a dozen coaches growing up. But brothers were different.

"Just beat up, I think. My head hurts like hell. Actually everything hurts, but I think I'm all right, mostly. I'd kill for some ibuprofen or something."

Aiden pulled out his water bottle and gave Josiah a drink, then produced four maroon pills and let Josiah swallow them. Next he pulled out an energy bar and tucked it into Josey's collar.

"Here. I'd give you something stronger but we can't let you get loopy yet, we're gonna have to get you on your feet soon. Sorry, I'm afraid I don't have any biscuits and gravy, either." He paused to let Josey absorb the joke, then got serious. "We're pretty screwed right now. Do you think you can walk, or do we need to put you on a stretcher?"

Josiah thought for a moment and tried to sit up, but fell backward into the sleeping bag. Hector and Aiden leaned forward but Josiah waved them off, "Sorry, I'm okay. Here, let me try that slower." He shifted onto his elbow and leaned up slowly into a sitting position. *Come on, suck it up, buttercup, these guys are your responsibility.*

His head still pounded, and he felt the wind whipping him again. The stinging in his eye numbed, he took his gloved hand and felt his face, eyes, and forehead. He shifted his legs, moved his hips, and felt around his body. Josiah looked up at Aiden and gave him a thumbs-up. Now he took the energy bar and tore it open with his teeth, discovering his fat split lip in the process, which made eating it all the worse. Slow bites, his jaw struggling to chew the cold, hard brick. The fake chocolate flavor had never tasted so good.

Aiden motioned for Hector, and with a nod he asked him to take over caring for his brother. Aiden gave Josiah a light squeeze on the shoulder and stood up and walked off toward the other shapes Josey hadn't even seen yet. He was becoming increasingly hungry. The first few bites had ignited his appetite and his body yearned for water and calories. Hector looked at Josiah. "Take it easy sir. I don't want you to throw it up. He's right, we're in a bit of a pickle, and you can't spare an ounce of fluid."

Josiah looked around and strained his good eye but barely saw a few dark figures standing about, a few others taking a knee in different directions. Josiah chewed and thought. He processed what he was seeing and he began to understand the predicament. He ticked off the facts as he knew them in his mind. *I'm sitting out in a snowstorm. Why? We must still be waiting for an evac helo. But they said we have to move, so this isn't the landing zone. A chopper can't land here, in this weather. Okay, so we need to move to a better spot. Probably need to wait for better weather. Visibility is...what, a few feet? Can they land in that? Maybe some can, I don't know. Probably not, so then we're cut off. The comms are probably down then too. Damn. Aiden's right. We better find some shelter and fast. Maybe that's what they mean.* He lay back and rested, then looked at Hector.

"You killed them?" he asked.

Hector was surprised. He was in patient-care mode, and hadn't thought at all about what had just happened in the cave. Certainly hadn't had time to process it. Hector had trained for it, but had never actually fired his weapon at an enemy. Now the realization came to him, and he had to think about what he had and hadn't done. "I didn't. They did," he said, nodding toward the others. "Sergeant McCoy took one out too."

Josiah turned his head to look toward his little brother, but couldn't see him. *Aiden bagged one of the bastards. Good.* Josiah knew his brother had wanted to save lives since they were young. He was always the first one by the side of a hurt kid on the playground. Aiden was the last person who would ever want to take a life, but Josiah knew that if his brother had pulled the trigger, he had done so intentionally, and would always have peace with the decision. Josiah loved his siblings, but he admired Aiden, and had told him so that Christmas Eve a thousand years ago.

—

Aiden moved over toward the mass of huddled shadows where Porter, Ray, and Andy were looking at the map. Porter looked up. "How is he? Looks like he's coming around."

Aiden nodded. "He'll be fine. He could use a rest but he says he can walk. What next?"

Porter and Andy went over the last communication from command: the previous landing zone was scrapped, as was the original one they had been heading for the day before when this circus had started. Both locations were deemed compromised and the brass didn't want to risk sending more birds into locations that were already well sighted by the enemy.

Porter tried not to think about what went into that decision, and instead decided to focus on things he could control. He had no desire to move in the direction they'd been ambushed at yesterday; but he had also seen the A-10 completely destroy that area. This mountain was obviously crawling with bad guys who were either just climbing out of their winter dens or never retreated into them in the first place. America's enemies were constantly adapting to her tactics— and getting harder to kill. But America was adapting as well, which is why some of its best men were currently in this place at this time.

Andy finally made up his mind. "It will take us at least three hours to get there, assuming it doesn't get worse. This storm is bipolar."

Several times the winds had stilled, the snow stopped, and the storm appeared to be clearing, only to have a gale-force wind kick up. The men stood ready for the next blast, getting colder, anxious, hungry, and pissed.

"Alright. Let's move out in five," Porter decided. He turned to Aiden, "We'll move as slow as we can. We've got time to kill probably, and I don't want to lose track of anybody on the way down. How are your men holding up?"

"Hundred percent. I'll tell them we're moving out." He started to walk off when he heard Porter's voice again.

"Gator owes you a beer, you know. Hell, I'll buy you one, too."

Aiden realized he was referring to the guy he'd killed. He hadn't given the matter a second thought; he was solely concerned with Josiah. He reflected on it for a half-second, and then shelved it away forever. He looked at Porter and replied simply, "Alright," and then turned.

Porter asked after him again, "You sure he can walk? We can carry him if we have to."

Aiden turned again. "He's tougher than he looks. He's my brother. If he says he can walk, he will."

Gator and Porter watched in stunned silence as Aiden walked off.

7

TEAMMATES

22:00:00
Afghanistan

The mountains of Afghanistan play havoc with radio communications on a clear day. With the snow, the wind, and the dense clouds, Andy was getting nothing. Since the failed extraction a few hours ago, he managed to get through exactly twice, and both times he was cut off prior to telling them any more than their call sign. While the team let Josiah rest and the PJs work, Andy kept at it and finally managed to get through with the good news.

"Rapier-One-Seven recovered. Request coordinates for extraction point." Dozens of people monitoring the net and trying to coordinate the rescue logistics felt a welcome relief. The pilots circling in F-16s overhead relaxed a little, still waiting in anticipation of the rescue choppers that would be coming as soon as they were able.

At the Raven headquarters there was an uneasy quiet. The radio call had not reported any casualties, which would have necessitated immediate and continuing calls, so they figured everyone on the ground was probably in good shape — but they were still on the ground. Speed, surprise, and stealth are prime ingredients for success in combat. In a perfect world, you swoop in, complete the mission faster than the bad guys can react, and get out before the dust settles. Every extra minute on the ground increases the likelihood of enemy contact. Every enemy contact increases the likelihood of friendly casualties. Every extra casualty increases the complexity of getting out and inevitably causes delays, which can lead to more casualties. This is how raids turn into battles, and battles sometimes turn into massacres.

There were SEALs at their base, PJs at their base, and pilots and ground crews at Josiah's base; all were aware their men were stuck on the ground, surrounded by sophisticated and heavily-armed enemies who were competent enough to take down a Warthog, tear up a Chinook, and shut down a landing zone. Time was going by incredibly slow. They'd all embarked on missions in terrible weather, and the weather at the various bases didn't seem noteworthy.

The pilots at the forward refueling station were wondering, too, eager for the green light. Chinook pilots had learned how little they knew the moment they began operating in the mountains of Afghanistan. They'd trained in cold mountainous regions in Alaska, Colorado, Canada; none of which were the same as the Hindu Kush mountains. But they had learned quickly. Training adapted their tactics and they learned how to work around the problems.

They waited. The order to head back up the mountain would come at any moment and they were poised and ready to go. They grumbled to themselves, certain they could fly in the current weather — had done so in the past— and knew that every minute mattered. Had they known that command had little idea where Polaris was, and still no clue where they might be able to secure a landing zone, they might have been less antsy, if not more troubled.

As it was, the two fully-fueled, fully-armed Chinooks were like sled dogs pulling against an anchored sled, jumping in their harnesses, snapping their teeth and barking at their masters to let the race begin. The PJs and flight crews on board anxiously fingered their weapons. Each checked and rechecked their various gear. Nobody could sleep, and only a few — the more experienced ones—had even tried. There was nothing to do but wait.

—

23:00:00

Matt, Hector, and Dave had a profound respect for Aiden, their quiet, determined, and talented leader. They had each partnered with him at various times in the back of a Blackhawk helicopter while he calmly saved lives amid shrapnel, turbulence, and broken equipment. They – especially Hector, who had met Josey once prior – would crawl over glass for him and his brother. Seeing Josey in person, hurt and in danger, gave them pause about their next course of action.

It was going to be a long, hard hike down the mountain in a snowstorm. Matt and Hector argued for a stretcher, tucked in from the wind and cold, so they could keep him on fluids. Dave said that would be impractical as the elevation and terrain would eventually cause him to get toppled over into the snow, and that all of the jostling would knock loose the IV anyway. Aiden simply told them that if Josiah wanted to walk, nobody was going to stop him. The fact that Josiah was already on his feet and asking which direction to go ended the debate.

The tight group of PJs parted for Porter as he moved into their circle and approached Josiah for the first time. "You all right to walk, Captain?" he asked.

"I'd rather take the slow tram and enjoy the view, but if you're all walking…then yeah, I'll manage it all right."

"Roger that, sir. We need to descend to a lower elevation, and try to secure a landing zone. Best estimate, it'll take around three hours to reach our target area." Porter looked around at the still falling snow. "May need to hunker down and make shelters. Any thoughts, sir?"

"This is your show, buddy. Just tell me who to follow," Josiah answered.

Porter pointed to Andy, who was already moving into the dark, followed by Ray. Josiah, pinned in by the PJs, moved in after them with Porter and Teddy taking up the rear.

Aiden waited for everyone to pass. It was his nature to be in the back of any line. He was always last to pick up a plate at a dinner buffet. He would stand in the back of a room with limited seating to make sure if someone was left without a chair, it would be him. At summer camps, he slept on the floor and let the other guys have the bunks; freely offered up his water; constantly doubled back on hikes to encourage stragglers. That Others May Live was a virtue he had lived out his entire life. He knew the last man in the line is often in greater need than the first.

It was a lesson first learned in high school basketball practice one hot Wednesday evening, when he was seventeen. Aiden was the fastest and best conditioned member of the team and naturally led the pack in every drill or workout. A month before the season began was Sweet Sixteen, sixteen days of three-a-day workouts beginning at 6:00 a.m. and ending at 6:00 p.m., consisting of countless miles of running, drills, and any other devices of torture the coaches could concoct, designed to thin the herd of varsity hopefuls. Somewhere around mile three of day seven, Aiden became team captain. He was about to lap the slowest member of the team, Jacob — a young, awkward, but talented sophomore who'd been encouraged by the coaches to compete for varsity— who was failing, and everyone knew it.

Aiden was filled with compassion as he passed the stumbling, gasping sophomore. Jacob was on the verge of collapsing in the hot sun. Just as Aiden pulled up next to him Jacob stopped, knelt down, and threw up. It was normal and Aiden knew that Jacob was not in danger — the trainers were always there — but Aiden had heard from others that Jacob was on the verge of quitting the team. He overheard the mocking in the locker room, but Jacob was no pushover and stood firm against the ridicule. Still, there was a pool going among the seniors as to which day of Sweet Sixteen Jacob would throw in the towel. It annoyed Aiden but he held his tongue. Like the coaches, he recognized Jacob's talent and he liked the quiet kid, hoped he would stick it out.

As he watched Jacob struggle on his knees on the sandy track, Aiden paused. Jacob slowly rose and began to walk instead of run, and Aiden knew, as did everyone else, that this would be Jacob's last lap on the varsity team. It bothered him.

After pondering it for a few paces, Aiden stopped, turned around, and walked up to him. He lifted his sunglasses and looked right into Jacob's surprised and bloodshot eyes, and quietly said, "You're going to make this team. You hear me, Jacob? I'll run with you. Come on, one step at a time. Let's go, slow and steady."

Giving Jacob no time to object, Aiden gently tugged on his elbow, and began a slow gentle jog. Jacob was hardly aware of what he was doing, but found it easier to pace alongside Aiden, who asked him questions every once in a while — the kind that didn't require long answers from the huffing and puffing sophomore. The rest of the team, especially the coaches, noticed as Aiden took the extra lap and a half at a snail pace. By the time the pair reached the final hundred meters, the entire team lined the track, clapping in time, encouraging Jacob, who was now running with his head up, smiling. Aiden ran faster and the two raced to the finish. To his amazement, Jacob didn't collapse, and he looked back toward Aiden with his head held high. Aiden didn't say anything else to Jacob at the finish. Just a high five, and then Aiden went off alone to the locker room. Nobody ever spoke of Jacob quitting again. Two years later, Jacob followed Aiden's lead again by joining the PJs.

Now, as Aiden watched the procession of men snake away down the cold mountain, he counted them off — eight men. *Wasn't there another one?* Just then Gator nudged him from behind. Aiden looked back and nodded, and Gator moved off alongside, equally determined that none of these PJs would fall behind. They moved down the dark path together, neither of them with any clear idea of what the next several hours would bring, but clinging to a hopeful expectation that very soon they would be in the air.

8

GUARDIAN

03:00:00
Afghanistan

Nobody but Porter knew it, but Gator was miserable. *I hate being cold,* he thought for the thousandth time since he first joined the Navy. Growing up in South Florida, Christopher L. Peterson — Gator— had spent his entire life in the warm glow of tropical breezes. Even the occasional hurricane was a soon-to-pass anomaly than never made him cold; the warm sun always eventually shone on his tanned skin like a smile from the pretty girl across the street. The warm Florida water was his oldest and best friend. He and his father surfed or fished from boats several times a week.

As he got older, he and his friends began skin diving with spears and homemade harpoons, the love of weapons gelling in him around the same age as most boys. His grandfather was a Navy veteran and a reader.

Gator's granddad told stories of war from the decks of ships, which whetted his appetite for more, eventually leading him to the tales of Vietnam-era SEALs and daring underwater missions. He and his buddies imagined swimming out to ships full of Russians and Cubans, taking them down, and saving Florida from invasion. The coast of Florida was the only ocean he had ever known. Then he got to the Pacific.

The day he arrived in San Diego he went straight to the beach, rented surfboard under his bare arm — he had never used a wetsuit, even at night— and walked confidently into the California waves. Cold water aggressively embraced his submerged feet, reached up through his spine, and slapped him across the face. From that day forward Gator decided to wage a personal war with cold. He was cold in his enlisted quarters on Coronado Island, California. In BUD/S training he had lain in the cold surf with waves breaking over his body day and night. He sat shivering in sand, desperately snuggling the men in front and behind him for what little body heat they could glean from each other.

He was always in the top five percent of any grouping he was part of, mainly because he considered every aspect of his training as a personal war between him and cold. He was cold whenever he went into a high-altitude parachute jump. He was cold in combat, cold in training — especially in that God-awful water in Sitka, Alaska — cold on the decks of ships, cold in the open sea for hours on end. Gator always used cold as a motivation to win, the human enemy an inconvenient side issue to deal with. His body had been trained into accepting and functioning through all but the final stages of hypothermia, but despite his abilities to endure it, he absolutely hated being cold.

Why in the world did these maniacs choose Afghanistan, Gator wondered. *There are plenty of warm places in the Middle East to hide. Plenty of jihadis in Asia. I could just as easily be killing them in Indonesia.* He didn't mind his time in those places. Many SEALs had done multiple missions in Iraq, but Gator always seemed to pull duty on some Afghan mountain. He had no problem sweating in the sun of Iraq or Africa, or in the jungles of the South Pacific, or in South America. He would gladly crawl for days through the muck and bugs of Somalia or Burma or wherever if it meant avoiding ever having to climb a mountain over 5,000 meters high in the winter. *People pay to do this for fun. Be warm. Buy a postcard.*

Yet here he was again; cold, miserable, pissed off. *Coffee. All I want in the world right now is coffee. Damn.* Gator saw Aiden moving slowly but confidently; allowed himself a brief moment to reflect on the ridiculous circumstances which brought them to this point. He moved on, hoping, knowing, they must be reaching their destination soon.

Everyone was in pain, Josiah by far the worst, but everyone struggled against the mountain's attempt to kill them, body and spirit. The physical strain was far beyond anything the PJs had experienced in war or peace. The SEALs were faring little better despite the familiarity with the terrain and their prior acclimation; they, too, were freezing. Everyone's lungs burned, heads ached, and vision blurred. They kept moving. They progressed with one heavy boot in front of the other, sinking to the knees in snow. Too tired to be irritable. They kept their heads down and only looked up briefly to confirm their bearings.

Initially the PJs' deep concern for Josiah garnered their attention. Now, seeing how well he was progressing, many of their nurturing tendencies threatened to evaporate, his survival seemingly at odds with their own. One thing kept bringing them back: That Others May Live. They repeated it to themselves with every creaky knee, every face-plant into the snow, and especially, every time they saw Josiah.

—

Every step for Josiah was a thousand agonies. Pain assaulted his head, ribs, back and face. It alerted him to his injuries and strangely gave him motivation. He hoped he wouldn't pass out from it. So many times he had wanted to raise his hand to try and stop the procession and break, but he knew they couldn't stop. He wouldn't stop even if he had to pass out and let them carry him. He was an officer, a captain, and he felt the weight of command, a responsibility for the lives of all these men who had put themselves in this awful place for him. He didn't beat himself up over getting shot down, since he knew he'd done everything right. The bad guys had just gotten in a good shot. It happens. None of the men were going to whine or plead for the mercy of a break. They all wanted it to end as quickly as possible, and so Josiah kept plugging along, praying this would end before he fell over and died.

—

Aiden and Gator kept watchful eyes on the line of men before them, both of them keenly aware of the danger of each man in tandem walking off into a similar death if they lost their way. There are frozen carcasses of men and women strewn about the peaks of this world, many a result of getting lost in the cold dark storms, their preserved bodies a testimony to man's frailty.

At the head of the column, Andy paused to check his GPS, then pulled out the laminated map and tried to reconcile the contour of the terrain around him with it. He shoved it back into his case in frustration, knowing that while the storm raged he was conducting educated guesswork at best. He looked back over his shoulder and made a few swift chopping motions with his right hand, reaffirming to Porter to carry on in the same direction. Andy was well aware they needed to secure the landing zone as fast as possible — if the weather cleared before they reached it, they would be exposed. There was no telling where the enemies were, and Porter's greatest fear was to be caught out in the open with no chance to prepare a defense.

Andy needed to get set up somewhere and establish good radio contact in order to direct an extraction, and if necessary, air cover. Getting the proper aircraft on station also took time; time that Andy was afraid they wouldn't have when the sun came out. They were like pioneers moving their wagons through a foggy canyon, praying their presence would go unnoticed by hostiles all around them.

Porter couldn't plan out how to secure it until they got there, and he knew they were likely to reach it completely exhausted, if not frostbitten. He would need to simultaneously get shelter and prepare to engage anything that might show up. They could do nothing while stumbling half-dead on their feet.

Missions such as these were the reason so many men

quit by ringing the bell at the SEAL training facility.
They graduated with a SEAL trident pinned to their
lapel because they were incapable of quitting, no matter
the circumstance. That training had completely taken
over. Self-preservation was silenced by years of
conditioning their long-since spent bodies.

———

Porter stumbled forward, straining to keep sight of
Andy and Ray. He noticed them standing erect, just
ahead. They were talking and making gestures. *If they
went and got us lost I'll kill them both right now*, Porter
thought. Ray abruptly turned, almost as if he'd heard
Porter's threat. He waved his hand at him and made a
sweeping gesture.

End of the line.

Thank God. Porter moved up toward them and
conferred, agreed. They had reached landing zone
Charlie. He looked around and saw nothing but falling,
gently blowing snow in every direction. It was dark.
Daylight visibility would not have been more than thirty
feet anyway, but at night, in these conditions, it was
impossible to see much of anything.   Ray and
Teddy moved off to the right a bit and crouched,
panning with their night vision to try to secure the
landing zone they couldn't even see. There might be a
thousand enemy fighters within a stone's throw and
neither side would know about it unless they happened
to stumble on top of each other. History is replete with
battles having begun thus; Porter hoped it would not be
the case tonight.

He turned to see the rest of the PJs pulling up
behind him. They, too, were exhausted, but upright and
waiting for the next step. "End of the line," he said with

a hint of irony.

Porter's gaze settled on Josiah, who was standing erect and looked more alert than any other man in the group except for Aiden. Porter wondered if it was simply the increased oxygen of the lower elevation working in the pilot's favor. *Or maybe it's something else.* He hoped they could get him a well-deserved rest soon, though Josiah didn't seem to need it as much as Porter did. *Maybe he's just relieved to still be alive*, he wondered and made a mental note to check in with him as soon as he had a chance.

———

For Josiah, the first mile had been grueling, but as it dragged on he could feel the mild increase of oxygen that accompanied the descent and his muscles started to respond. His brain began to send messages to his body, to call up reserves, but what really brought him back to life was that he began to think. Many of his best ideas and solutions came to him in the midst of a physical exertion. Sometimes he would daydream, or draft a letter to his wife. Sometimes he would make compositions or reports in his head, the time and the miles disappearing in the focus. You could call it "the zone," but Josiah hated that term. He merely became contemplative, and he'd spent the better part of the last three hours in contemplation.

He thought about the men around him; realized that if they didn't get picked up soon, eventually he would have to assert his rank and assume leadership of the situation. Josiah was not intimidated by it, but wondered how it would play out. For all of his years in the Air Force, he had never spent time with SEALs and wondered how things would go down if he had to start making decisions for them all.

It struck him that maybe he was wrong about the entire situation. Perhaps he had no command responsibility in this situation; certainly he had no knowledge or experience to offer. Maybe he was supposed to just walk and keep his mouth shut. He couldn't remember the rules. Is my brain just going nutso? he wondered. *Sleep, that would be helpful. Or would it? Do I have a concussion? Stop thinking about it, Josey. Just take one thing at a time.* On and on it went in his mind, hour after hour, mile after mile, until the answers came into focus at about the same time the procession stopped.

———

Aiden and Gator walked side by side, each wanting to keep an eye on the last man in the line and not wanting to move too far ahead. Around an hour ago something unspoken gelled in them, and they began keeping perfect pace with one another. A couple of times they noticed a man veer off the trail, and one of them had to rush off to put him back in line. Several were experiencing hallucinations. Every so often, one of the men thought he saw lights of a cabin, or maybe a helicopter. Aiden moved with slow confidence. He and Gator gave each other quick looks and small gestures in lieu of words. With each step their silent respect for one another increased.

Gator was impressed at how well conditioned the Air Force guys seemed to be and how well they seemed to stay on task. He'd had mixed experience with Coalition troops. He had proper respect for Army guys and Marines, but he'd also met some real tools and seen things go awry by bad tactics and worse commanders.

You never knew what to expect from guys you didn't know till it was too late. Gator had trained with Norwegian, British, and Australian Special Forces and was amazed to find that they met — and sometimes exceeded — SEAL standards. Regular Army, Rangers, Marines, he was familiar with, and though he didn't really rely on them, they at least spoke the same language. Air Force pilots however, guys who flew fast movers with soft hands, he had no clue what they were made of. Most of the PJs and corpsmen he'd met were mild mannered; not the kind of guys who get into bar fights, the polar opposite of SEALs. And though he knew they were certainly talented in the medical field, he had no idea what to expect from a PJ in a fight. He looked at Aiden, and liked him, but wondered.

———

As soon as the word spread that the landing zone was secure, Porter put everyone to work. They needed to dig into a snow bank, carving out an ice cave to provide some concealment and shelter from the wind.

Andy tried all of his radios for a good signal into any of the aircraft he knew were up there, but was locked in a losing battle with geography and meteorology. Through broken transmissions he managed to establish confirmation of their location, their hold status, and health, and was instructed to stand by.

Teddy paced back and forth, looking for any indication of obstacles to a helo landing. He would have liked a little daylight to secure the site, since the snow could mask rocks and ice and even with night vision it was near impossible to get a command of the terrain in the dark. There could be hidden enemy structures as well. He'd seen enough aircraft shot up in the last several hours from bad guys who seemed to come out of nowhere.

———

Aiden checked up on Josey, and then rejoined Gator. Porter approached them. "You gonna fire up the grill and cook some ribs? We're stuck here till God knows when," he said. "Andy says we may as well get comfortable."

Gator glanced at Aiden, "Don't suppose you brought some burgers with you?"

Aiden smiled. "Sorry, just cold pork and beans, bro."

"That'll do fine by me. Let's get some shelter though." Gator motioned over where the others had dug out two spacious caves that could each accommodate three men and their gear. Josiah was laying down in one with Hector monitoring him. Ray and Dave were sharing MREs in the other. Aiden and Gator got to work digging their own.

———

Josiah was propped up on his elbow, chewing something; even he didn't know what it was. Porter plopped down next to him. "I don't imagine you guys have to settle for MREs very often in your line of work, huh?" he asked.

"No," Josiah smiled, "We've usually got it pretty good. This week's been a bit of an exception to the rule. I'll have to make a note to not get my keester shot down anymore. It's rather hard on the body, worse on the ego." He chuckled.

Porter smiled, took a bite of his own meager dinner.

"I'm sorry we got you into this mess, Captain. Wish we could have gotten to you before they did."

Both of them ate some more, waiting for the other to break the ice. Finally Josiah said, "Thanks for coming after me. I don't know how you found me, though, I thought I was dead for sure. "

Porter looked Josiah in the eye. "Captain, when you get back to your squadron, let those guys know we'll go to the ends of the earth to bring y'all back. So don't ever quit on yourself."

"I will most certainly let them know that."

Porter took another bite. When he finished chewing he reached into the inner pocket of his jacket and pulled out the holstered Browning pistol and handed it to Josiah, said "I would have given this to you earlier, but you were pretty out of it. Hopefully you won't need it today."

Josiah looked at the pistol and felt his heart bump in his chest, followed by the realization that he'd almost lost it. He tried to fight it but tears welled nonetheless. He felt both relief and guilt at the same time; he hadn't thought about the gun since he was preparing to use it a day earlier. Now, seeing it safe and realizing it had been lost caused him to feel momentarily terrified, like realizing you'd escaped a car accident by mere seconds. Josiah looked at the precious gift through watery eyes and worried about the men on the choppers who'd been coming for him. Wondered what had happened but realized Porter might not even know. Decided not to go there just yet.

Instead, he looked at the younger, tougher man who'd had the presence of mind to retrieve it for him, and was gratefully humbled.

"Thank you." Josiah couldn't think of anything else to say.

Porter knew there must be a story in there. He'd put a pin in it and bring it up over a beer someday, if they ever got the chance.

After watching Porter take a few more bites, Josiah said, "I know Aiden and his guys are PJs. You Navy? I'm sorry, I don't remember your name."

"That's because I never told you. Lieutenant Peter S. Dawkins, US Navy, sir. You can call me Porter though."

"Don't like Peter?" Josiah asked.

"It's not that, sir. In the teams we often use nicknames. It's just easier."

"So why Porter?"

"I like good beer. These rednecks from the sticks, and these surfer punks like Gator over there wouldn't know a good beer from a bottle of dip spit. I spent months when I first joined the teams drinking the watered-down swill that these kids would buy. Eventually I got fed up with their MGD and their Coors crap and I started bringing in a decent pack of my own for the fridge. They drink it all up, but every one of them knows to leave me at least one, because the last guy who didn't — well, he was sorry he didn't. Anyway, that's me."

"Well," Josiah began, "when we get back home and I take your team out for a drink, I'll let you choose the tap."

"Sounds like a plan, Captain."

They ate quietly for another few minutes before Porter asked, "I didn't realize the sergeant was your brother. Ironic he got pegged for this mission, huh? How's that gonna play around the kitchen table at Thanksgiving?"

Josiah rolled his eyes and nodded. "Yeah, he'll have fun with it eventually, but overall he's pretty quiet. My wife will probably make me pay for it more."

"Yeah, I noticed the quiet part," Porter agreed. "Let them know they should be proud of him though. He handled himself as good as any of my guys in that hole. It's no easy thing to go in and perform like they did. We're trained for it, but they can surprise you, I guess. Your brother's a good field commander."

"Yes, yes he is, Lieutenant. He's been surprising me my whole life."

Porter smiled, "So, where you from?"

—

Gator was half sitting, half lying on his pack, trying his best to find a position that would allow him to rest without exposing his core to the ice. Teddy took up so much of the space. It was futile, and he'd just acknowledged as much to himself when he noticed Aiden moving back and forth to the various men sheltering as best they could in the ice caves — a survival tool they'd all learned at one time or another in training, and were now glad they had. Dave, Ray, and Hector were farther off, appearing to be trying to sleep, and Andy was still messing with his radios every ten minutes or so, in between bites. The SEALs were taking turns scanning the perimeter with their night vision.

Gator was sitting in the shelter Aiden had helped him and Teddy carve before making his rounds. Gator called to him. "Hey Bro, take it on advice, you should rest up. Nothing's gonna happen for awhile. Save your strength and get charged up because if it hits the fan later you'll need it. Come here."

Aiden was anxious for his men and especially for Josiah, and had checked to see if anyone was injured or ill. He was most concerned with frostbite and hypothermia, but everyone seemed to be functioning as well as could be expected under the circumstances. He wanted to sit down with Josiah but noticed that his brother was talking with one of the SEALs and decided not to interrupt. He was getting very cold, but having grown up in it he was used to subzero temps. He'd played hockey on frozen ponds in minus-three degrees for hours as a teenager. He and his sister would often have to be dragged in by mom at meal times. Neither of them minded the cold; they could disconnect it and accept it as a backdrop that would not affect their plans for the day. It was one of the lessons he and his siblings had learned from their father: *Rarely do you get to choose the circumstances, but you can always choose your attitude.* He was determined to use the time allotted to him to prepare his men for whatever lay ahead. But he was tired, and admit it or not, he needed shelter from the biting wind. With mild reluctance he squeezed into what room remained next to Gator, and immediately felt the relief of the protection from the elements.

"Thanks, you're right," Aiden said as he looked back and saw Teddy's hulking frame, sleeping like a baby.

"Here, want some chow?" Gator handed him the opened package of food, and Aiden took out a pack of crackers and some peanut butter. The MRE packets were full of items high on calories, low on flavor and pizazz. They worked, but always left one pining for something more. Aiden reached into the cargo pocket of his pant leg and pulled out a small plastic bottle. The energy drink was little more than a shot of pure caffeine, but he and his fellow PJs lived on the things, especially when they were on the night shift rotations and he'd developed a habit of keeping a couple on him as standard gear. Right next to his scissors. Aiden handed the second bottle to Gator.

"And now I love PJs," Gator said. "Thanks."

They downed their shots, then looked at each other and saw the first smile either of them had given in the last 24 hours.

"We live off those things," Aiden said with a laugh. "Works better than morphine practically, too." He peeked out and looked at the other man sleeping in the darkness, and wondered about the four bearded men he was following. "How did you guys get wrapped up in this mess?" he asked.

Gator started cleaning ice out of his rifle and didn't look up as he spoke. "We were on our way to our extraction LZ when we got ambushed. Your brother was flying close air support for us when he got hit. When we saw him go down, we went after him. You know the rest."

"How'd he get shot down?" Aiden had been wondering.

"No idea. We just saw his wing come off and he started spinning; some sort of MANPAD maybe. I don't think it was a missile, but who knows. The hajis have all sorts of stuff up here."

Aiden asked, "What were you doing here?"

Gator looked up and stared at Aiden. He thought about his mission, the nature of classification; measured how much he could tell this stranger, then he remembered the rat hole. He already knows all about it anyway. Hell, he got one of the dudes himself. Gator figured that made him part of Polaris by all accounts.

"We were sent here to watch that cave, the one we found him in. We'd been sitting on it for two weeks waiting for them to have a party so we could crash it, or bomb the crap out of it. There was never much going on there, though. Every so often a few guys would hole up there for a night, not worth the effort. It was all BS anyway, though."

"How's that?" Aiden asked.

"We were set up. There was this little Afghan that led us up there. He was supposedly familiar with the area and turned. The intel guys said he checked out, but he was dirty. We knew it the minute we set eyes on him. Teddy looked at me and we both shook our heads. I don't trust any of these guys anymore, but this was definitely dirty from the get-go."

Aiden nodded knowingly. "Yeah, we've got a lot of that blue on green stuff where we operate. A lot of the time when we go wheels down, the Afghans, they just rush up toward the chopper and we have to shoo them off and threaten to pop them. They just walk straight up to us like morons who want to get killed. Most of them are just ignorant, but you never know."

Gator nodded. "Well, we knew this time. This guy was going to try and screw us. We were positive, Porter too— that's the Lieutenant — anyway as soon as we got on the ground, Porter took his rifle and shoved it into the dude's back and told him to lead the way. Let him know that if he did anything other than walk slowly he'd shoot him in a heartbeat. That seemed to sober him. Kept saying how much he loved Americans. At one point, Teddy there grabbed him by the beard and told him that if anything happened he would be the first one to die. He was terrified, which was good for us, but we watched him like a hawk just in case. Later the bosses called off the mission and were about to pull us out when Haji's buddies showed up. They must have had an ambush all set up because he led us straight into it," Gator slammed a magazine back into his rifle and set it down.

"So you took him out?" Aiden asked.

"He tried to run off after the first shots, but Ray hit him from behind. It got ugly after that. We were pinned down so Andy called in an airstrike. Your brother torched them with a few passes and it looked all good, then we saw him go down. Sure as hell saved our skinnies. I love those ugly Warthogs."

"I'm sure we'll see a couple as soon as the sky clears," Aiden said.

"We'll see. I don't know, these mountains can be as desolate as the moon one second, and the next it's like the mountain walls open up or something and a thousand pissed off bad guys pop out of nowhere. I hate this place. Sorry. I'm not usually this much of a jerk but I haven't had coffee for two weeks." Gator grinned.

"Not a skier, I take it," Aiden laughed. "Where are you from, then?"

"Florida, where civilized people go to retire and die, because it's warm. I never got used to being cold," Gator said.

Aiden smiled, "Well, that explains it."

Gator laughed back. "Hey, get me on the desert sand and I'm your huckleberry. I just don't dig the cold. Try and get some sleep, we're not going anywhere for at least a couple of hours."

"Probably should have waited on this, then." Aiden looked at the empty bottle in his hand.

"You're right. Oh well, I'll try anyway. Wake me if you find any coffee and pancakes in that pack of yours, all right?" Gator said. He lay back and huddled into his collar.

Aiden debated closing his eyes for a second. Then he looked around, got back up, and started another round to check on the rest of the eight men sitting, waiting, sleeping, dreaming about getting home. He would close his eyes when they were all secured. Till then he'd keep watch.

Gator watched him walk off with a half-opened right eye and smiled, then went back to sleep thinking, *Our guardian.*

9

THE GOLDEN HOUR

The Golden Hour: The hour immediately following traumatic injury in which medical treatment to prevent irreversible internal damage and optimize the chance of survival is most effective.

04:00:00
Afghanistan

The world was purple. The breaking daylight of the approaching dawn filtered through the clouds and snow of the dissipating storm. Above the clouds, mountain peaks emerged from the blanket of white powder, the sun about an hour away from revealing what the storm had left across the range. The pilots circling the mountains finally got their first glimpse of the target they might soon be asked to attack. They were the first to know that the end was about to begin.

19:00:00 EDT
US Special Operations Command, Florida

General DeBerg looked over the papers on his desk. The first casualty of the operation had been confirmed. He read the name, Jason Holmes, the Raven door gunner who had just died in surgery at Bagram Joint Theater Hospital at Bagram Air Field. He silently said a prayer for the man's family. *Jesus, let them find peace, and let us honor his sacrifice.* Then he moved on to the next stack of intel.

Weather reports were good. The storm was ending and there would be a window very soon, possibly within the hour, where the choppers could go in and extract the last men from Operation Trap Line. The clock on his computer monitor gave the hour in four separate time zones, and he looked at the one labeled Kabul. *Just past four in the morning,* he thought. *Getting light soon.* He'd hoped to be able to give the green light while it was still dark. They owned night operations — get in and out before they all wake up. *More bad luck.*

He looked at the picture of his oldest daughter and her fiancé on his desk, and remembered when she was a little girl. She had decided to marry a soldier like her mom did; her fiancé was an Army paratrooper. DeBerg liked him and wondered if his future son-in-law would ever be in a situation like this, and how he would ever tell his little girl if her husband didn't make it out. Maybe there was a young lady waiting to hear from Jason Holmes. Instead, she would be greeted with an Army officer and a grief counselor. DeBerg would find out about the family, compose a letter himself. He always thought such letters were cold and detached attempts of assuaging one's guilt. But families always appreciated them, and so, even though he always felt like a jerk writing them, he always did. *God, let there be only one letter to write today.* He got up and moved down the hallway to the operations center.

—

04:45:00
Hindu Kush Range, Afghanistan: Landing Zone Charlie

Andy began hearing clear communications before he even noticed the clouds parting. He confirmed his information with the AWACS plane circling up in the stratosphere, who further confirmed it to the Raven headquarters, who passed it on to the Chinook pilots sitting on the helipad on the FARC at the base of the mountain. The engines on two helicopters started turning the twin-rotors and in less than two minutes they were in the air.

—

Andy was finally excited. He walked over to Porter to deliver the good news. "They're inbound. ETA seven minutes."

"Let's get on with it," Porter said. He took in the contours of the land just beginning to take shape in the waning dark. There was a gentle breeze blowing, a faint tickle on the collars of the men who'd spent the last several hours trying and failing to keep the stinging wind from licking exposed flesh in their cramped snow shelters.

What had been fierce wind a few hours ago had abated to mild gusts that washed away the snow-filled clouds and increased visibility to full. The diverse group of men looked each other over for the first time in the increasing daylight as they brushed five inches of snow off their gear, packs and weapons, preparing to depart.

Aiden checked to make sure he hadn't left anything on the ground or in the ice cavern. He surveyed his men doing likewise; shouldering weapons, stamping their feet, stretching out the kinks from muscles that had been sitting on ice all night. He looked and saw Josiah crouching between Hector and Dave, as if trying to stay out of the way. *Good*, Aiden thought. *Let us get you out of here.*

Instinctively Aiden looked up to the sky and noticed something didn't seem quite right, something he hadn't seen in a long time — stars, beaming from behind the scattered clouds, brilliant, beautiful. Aiden loved stars. For a moment he was a child again, lying on his back in the bed of his dad's pickup, huddled together in snow pants and down jackets on clear, cold winter nights, brothers and sisters packed in tight around him, all on top of Dad who interspersed stories with astronomy lessons. He taught them how to spot satellites, and the difference between planets and stars, star clusters and constellations. Aiden always felt simultaneously like a peon and a titan looking at that glorious celestial canvas.

The mountain's beauty captivated him and he realized that men climb mountains for mornings such as these. His present circumstance was such a strange contradiction, so much beauty and so much danger coexisting. It was counterintuitive but he allowed himself to enjoy the view, brief though it was.

He looked back down at the men around him and came back to reality. *Look sharp. Complete the mission.* At the same moment, a sound broke through the silence of the crisp morning air.

Helicopters. Here they come.

Clearly heard but still unseen flew two Chinooks,

and high above them, an AC-130 Spectre gunship, and even higher, two F-16 Falcons. It was still dark enough that the painted hull of the massive Chinook blended in well with the mountainside, a defensive design that made it harder for an enemy to see the aircraft, and the reason why choppers preferred to operate at night. But, it was no longer night. All were silently praying or hoping that the chopper would emerge any second and put down.

Then they saw it.

The beautiful helicopter came straight toward them, low on the horizon. Each man dared to hope it would all be over soon. As the sound of the rotors became more intense, they instinctively looked at it, then down again, panning the horizon 360 degrees for any enemy movement. Suddenly, their eyes were drawn again as yellow flashes emanated from the side of the chopper, its left side door gunner firing into the snow, interrupting the peace of daybreak.

The sounds of the guns reached them a second later, and they saw tracer rounds coming up from higher up the mountain, from a large grouping of rocks they were unable to see thirty minutes ago. The tracers pounded the Chinook and it pitched wildly to avoid ground fire. The Spectre gunship unloaded a barrage on the location of the tracer fire's origin and began a slow turn. Flares poured out of its tail section in an attempt to trick anti-aircraft missiles that must have been detected by its computer.

At the same moment an explosion hit the lead chopper. Smoke billowed from the left engine, blocking out the stars. It climbed, trying desperately to stay in the air, spinning to the left and gaining altitude and moving away from them.

The second chopper attempted to come in firing but

quickly turned away to gain altitude, and then appeared to be circling. The Spectre came in again and started to pound a different area, but then took evasive maneuvers. Everything stopped as suddenly as it had begun.

The few moments felt like a lifetime from the ground. The gunship was circling and the choppers had backed off. The eyes in the air searched, scanning everywhere for targets, and both sides knew it. The enemy, so well concealed, was smart enough to keep their heads down till the choppers were in range. But the attempt to land had also alerted them to the presence of the men on the ground waiting for the choppers.

———

All Porter could do was watch and wait. He saw the choppers in the distance and heard Andy communicating with the gunship. Andy was as calm and collected as Porter had ever heard him, in his element now, running the show with his assortment of radios and years of training. Combat air controllers are some of the most valuable assets a ground force can have, and Porter was always impressed with what they could accomplish in turning a battle around. It was Andy's show now.

He spoke with two F-16 fighters, giving them coordinates for a possible bomb release onto the grid the Spectre had fired on. But nobody could see the bad guys. The Spectre was searching with long range cameras to spot targets, but all it saw was snow and rocks.

Porter knelt next to him to listen in. Andy debated

with himself whether or not to drop a few bombs before trying another run at the choppers, who at this altitude were burning fuel quickly.

Josiah moved up close behind Andy, fascinated by seeing close air support from the ground perspective. He was so used to the other end of this scenario that he was caught completely off guard by what it looked like from here – the words were familiar, but he had never seen them spoken before. He was used to hearing the instructions and the requests on the radio. It was quiet for a few moments and Andy began to speak to the Chalk 2 Chinook pilot, still circling, when the comforting drone of high altitude fighters was broken up by crackling sounds, and the high pitched whine of an incoming RPG round.

The rifle fire reached their ears before the bullets or the RPG. All of a sudden everyone's senses were assaulted by a world of explosions, seemingly from all sides.

The RPG broke the rocks behind them, showering them with mostly snow and dirt. Every man hit the deck or took a knee behind whatever cover was available. Ray was close to Teddy and both began firing at the direction of the RPG. Half a dozen shadows moved behind the rocks above and to the northwest. Suddenly they peeked out from behind the rocks and sprayed wildly with their AK-47s. The snow all around began to erupt with AK rounds. The PJs and SEALs fired short bursts towards the rocks above them.

Josiah pulled out his pistol and aimed it in the same direction, and then realized the range was more or less worthless for him with a handgun. *Save the ammo for what you can hit,* he told himself. Still, he kept it aimed at the rocks.

Several rounds hit the ground to the left of him and

he flinched and closed his eyes, then fell down and rolled over, trying to get his arms under him to see what was happening. He brushed the snow away from his face and saw that it was stained red. *Am I hit?* He felt his body, looked around but didn't feel anything, then he looked to his left and a chill ran down his spine.

Andy was crumpled over on his side, blood spreading onto the snow beneath him, the warmth of it digging a hole in the fresh snow. Josiah wanted to be sick but there was no time. He pushed Andy over to see if he could help him and was immediately pushed over roughly onto his backside. Aiden was there.

"Get down, Josey," his little brother demanded.

Aiden was straddling Andy before Josiah even had time to comprehend what happened. Aiden looked Andy over quickly, then moved his upper body off further to the left and rolled him over. In a flash, he removed Andy's radio pack and lunged back to where Josiah was lying.

"He's dead, Josey. Here, get on it and get us some air support on that ridge. Hurry, run over to that snowbank. We're too exposed here. I'll cover you. Move!"

With that Aiden had his rifle up and was pouring fire into the direction of the shots. Josey couldn't see what they were firing at, and didn't look to find out. He picked up the radio pack, and immediately fell forward when he tried to scoop it up, not realizing how heavy was with all of its batteries. Porter pulled him by the collar of his flight suit while Josiah gave it a second effort, adjusting for the weight, and they darted to the snow bank twenty feet to the right.

The low, packed snow didn't provide much cover. Josiah face-planted into it and cradled the precious radio. He got back to his knees and crouched as he scooted the rest of the way, Porter continuing to shield and pull him as he fell into place. Porter landed on top of him and had his knee in Josiah's back as he started shooting.

"Get us some air cover, Captain. You've got the comms now. Tell your buddies to fry 'em," Porter instructed without looking away from the battle, kneeling and swinging left and right, shooting slowly, methodically in short bursts.

Josiah picked up the phone and put it to his ear. He called out to anyone listening and was immediately in contact with the F-16. Josiah didn't know the process from this end, but he knew what the pilots needed to hear. He guided the F-16 in from the same direction the chopper had approached. "Guns only. Danger close," he warned the pilot.

"Roger that, incoming," the pilot warned.

"Incoming, get down!" Josiah hollered, hoping that the eight men who were scattered around would all hear and heed the warning.

They all covered their heads with their arms and waited for long seconds before hearing the sharp pings of the 20mm rounds pounding into the rocks and snow. The fighter pulled up and turned after making the pass, allowing a mere few seconds of peace before the shooting continued.

Josiah's heart sank. He'd expected the strafing to silence the ridge. That was what it was supposed to do. How could anyone live through that onslaught? Josiah lifted the phone to his ear, ready to try again, wondering how many more passes it would take to subdue this mountain.

05:30:00

The low fog at sunrise obscured the portion of the mountain directly across from them. They had no idea what was near other than rocks, which they could not see but had assumed were there. Now the fog had burned off, the sun just beaming over the range and lighting up the landing zone in streams that were disorienting and blinding at times.

For the first time they realized how awful their ground was. Directly in front of them, elevated by eleven feet was a long line of jagged tooth-like rocks. They could see no approaches up and into them. It was as perfect a position to fire down from as a castle wall.

Ray, Teddy, Matt, and Hector huddled down in the snow, lying on their stomachs, trying to hit something as enemies peered around rock parapets and sprayed inaccurate rifle fire. About ten meters to their right, Gator and Dave were shooting at the now exposed tree line. Neither man could see anyone among the trees but they knew there was fire coming from that direction.

Porter and Josiah were back about ten feet, equidistant from both groups of men, and with slightly more cover. The enemy was taking full advantage of a well-concealed, elevated position from one side, and the trees from another, and seemed to multiply before their very eyes. The clearing in both directions was too vast for the men to properly assault. They would be exposed the entire way. It would be up to the Air Force to subdue the attackers before a chopper could land. They were running out of time.

Aiden was still kneeling over Andy. He felt around the body for any sign of life. Aiden had known the man was dead as soon as he'd seen him, yet had learned to always hold out hope despite the gore — no matter how flimsy that hope may be— because maybe, just maybe, something might be done.

But Andy was dead.

Throughout all of his deployments, Aiden had only lost three men in the field; now he had lost a fourth. All PJs carry a carefully folded American flag in their gear to cover a fallen soldier with if the need arises; a final show of respect. Aiden would have to wait until they were safely aboard the chopper before he could do so. The firefight was raging.

Aiden looked around. They were firing sporadically with carefully aimed shots, and the volume of incoming fire had diminished. *For how long*, he wondered. He looked over the men again; men he knew, now fighting alongside relative strangers, yet already had a sense of connection with them. Aiden considered them all — Andy included — his men, and he was going to get the rest home safe or die trying. And then there was Josiah. Aiden looked back down at Andy. Something began to stir in Aiden: a blend of anger, mixed with frustration and stubbornness.

That others may live.

Nine men, he counted. He looked at Josey again; a lingering memory from that awful day when they were kids resurfaced in the pit of his stomach. The resolve he'd made to himself as a child came back, moved into his chest, and surged through his legs and arms.

Aiden remembered something his father told him on the day of his first deployment ceremony. After the tearful hugs from his mother and little sisters, his father looked him in the eye and seemed lost for words. Tears threatened to overwhelm both men before his dad managed to say, "Son, I'm sorry that I don't know what to tell you. You know I've never served in the military. I have no idea what combat is like because I've never been near one, I've only read about them. I don't have anything to teach you about what you are about to face. So all I have to say about it is this. Whatever you are faced with over there, whatever decision you find yourself having to make, just always make sure that you can live with the outcome. You'll have to live with the consequences. Make sure that you'll be able to look at yourself in the mirror, for the rest of your life, and be able to say that you did everything you could – that you didn't leave anything on the bench."

That others may live.

Aiden picked up Andy's rifle and ran over to Josiah and Porter. "Here," he said as he laid the rifle next to Josey.

Josiah was on the radio walking in another fighter toward the ridge for another strafing run. He nodded in recognition, his eyes conveying understanding and weariness. Aiden looked over the snow bank and saw two of his PJs and a pair of SEALs kneeling, looking at the rocks above them. Dave and Matt were side by side. To the right of Matt, the massive hulk of Teddy was patiently firing single shots, aimed and steady. On the left of Dave was Ray, also cautious with his diminishing ammo. He was lying down with his sniper rifle, watching men fall backwards in his scope with every shot, noticing that a man would eventually emerge from the same spot a few seconds later, but it was always a different man. Ray glanced up and caught the movement of a shape behind one of the rocks.

Aiden saw the figure at the same time as Ray. The figure lifted a launch tube to his shoulder. Aiden leapt up, pointed at the rocks and shouted, "RPG!"

Just as he mouthed the word, the rocket flew with a trail of smoke covering the expanse toward the four Americans. A jarring explosion preceded the shower of debris, followed by a sickening scent as all four men were tossed aside like bowling pins; then, a scream of pain, followed by swearing.

Aiden was up and over the snow bank running toward the site before the first cries of, Corpsman!" rang out.

Porter watched the PJ as he ran straight into a shower of rifle fire. Porter started pouring into the position, trying to cover Aiden. Josiah dropped the radio receiver and picked up the rifle and followed suit, almost standing, hoping to draw fire away from his little brother when Porter yanked him back down and yelled at him, "Captain! I got this, get 'em to hit that damned ridge again."

Aiden ignored the bullets kicking up around him. All that existed were the scattered men in front of him. He immediately began categorizing the three who were rolling around. In the split second it took him to cover the distance he was able to determine that Teddy and Dave were merely shaken up, and Matt was injured and bleeding from his arm but didn't appear to be critically so. Ray, however, was a bloody mess.

Priority, CAT-5...crap, he thought. Aiden didn't know Ray's name; couldn't remember if he had learned it earlier but wished he had. Ray's arm was severed below the elbow, bone slightly protruding from the mass of tissue that had been his forearm. Aiden worked fast.

Though he wouldn't say he was used to the shock and sight of mangled bodies and death, he had learned how to focus on the problem and push the traumatic sights to a box in the back of his mind. He wondered if someday they would come back to haunt him; had heard stories of nightmares for years to come, but he'd never had that happen. He figured if it ever did he'd just deal with them when the time came. It was just part of the job he signed up for because it was what he had wanted to do since he was seventeen. *That others may live.*

Aiden pulled out a handmade tourniquet, webbing, and a small dowel rod. He had four of them in his gear alongside the standard equipment, two large and two smaller ones. He picked the smaller version for arms versus the larger ones for thighs or legs. The PJs all had several in their gear, but Aiden preferred his custom homemade versions. The SEAL no doubt had one in his leg pocket as well, and ordinarily a medic would pull out the injured man's first aid pack and use it on him, saving his own bandages and equipment as a reserve for other injuries.

This time though, Aiden decided to use the version he most trusted. He rammed his left thumb into the pressure point in Ray's elbow, desperate to hold the bleeding in check until he could get out the tourniquet with his free right hand. He knew the exact pocket each piece of gear was in and had it out in no time, maneuvering it around and whipping the webbing around Ray's arm, then sticking the dowel rod through the open loop and cranking it like a corkscrew.

Aiden had practiced this a thousand times, first on stuffed animals, then on his little sister — he'd spent a week off desserts as punishment for that little experiment — then on himself before moving on to dummies, and finally, in combat operations for the past several years.

As he worked, he sensed Teddy and Dave had recovered and were shooting next to him. It was a strangely comforting feeling, as was the shrieking sound of a fighter jet coming in for another strafing pass. Aiden didn't see any of it; was focused on his patient as he watched the bleeding slow, and he released the pressure point. He grabbed the bandages and tape out of his other pocket to wrap it up and seal it off. Dave came behind him, offering assistance, and Aiden was about to have him set Ray up with an IV when he noticed blood dripping off Dave's arm.

"Dave, you're hit," he said.

Dave looked at his arm, ran his other hand along his bicep and winced when his fingers touched the piece of shrapnel, igniting pain from the nerve endings that were being sadistically tickled by the jagged piece of Russian-made metal embedded in his arm.

"It's not bad," he lied, through gritted teeth. Compared to Ray, he was right. It wasn't that bad, but the pain made his heart rate red-line and he got light headed. He shook it off.

Matt was back up and helping Teddy cover the PJs as they worked on Ray. Teddy looked over periodically and said, "Hang in there RayRay. He'll patch you up good as new."

Ray was fading in and out of a shock-induced fog. He had perfect clarity one second, with the full sensation of pain and Aiden's hands treating him, and then would slowly drift into a separate realm where everything was muted like a dream, only to be thrust back again as if being slapped or dunked into ice water. Ray knew what was happening to him, knew his arm was gone, knew he would probably be dead soon unless they got medevac'd. Fear began to sweep through him. He looked around and reached for his rifle with his good arm. He cradled it and then felt himself being lifted.

"Let's move him over there." Aiden pointed to show Dave an area that seemed to provide a little more cover. Matt was holding his own bleeding arm and moved next to Aiden, who didn't look up, but recalled the priority he'd assigned to the various injuries earlier. "You good?" he asked. "How's that arm?"

"Nothing. We moving him?" Matt knew he probably needed several stitches at the very least but would have to wait on that. The PJ's were already ticking off the minutes, knowing full well the golden hour had begun.

Each passing minute diminished Ray's chances of survival; the first hour of a trauma was critical. With the right care, a patient could become stable and the life-saving measures would hold for the time needed to get him in for serious medical attention, surgery, or whatever was needed. Aiden knew the clock was ticking, but also knew it was unlikely that a chopper could land soon, much less make the trip back to any friendly hospital within that time. It was up to him to keep Ray alive, alert. He wouldn't let him slip away, no matter how long they were stuck here.

"Matt and I will carry him," Aiden informed Dave and Teddy, then looked at Teddy, "Cover us."

"I got you," Teddy yelled then turned and began firing rapidly. "Go!"

Dave followed suit, and Aiden and Matt pulled Ray up. Aiden held him under the arms and Matt grabbed his legs. Matt began running at a pace Aiden wasn't ready for and he almost dropped him, his blood-soaked gloves sliding under the man's weight. Aiden managed to get his fingers locked inside Ray's opened pocket zipper for extra friction and a better grip and yanked him up. The two PJs covered the distance to the area Aiden had pointed to, just a few feet past Josiah and Porter's position. They were just about to take cover behind a decent-sized rock when Matt fell forward with a thud and crunched into the snow. Aiden slammed into Ray's shoulder and fell on top of him.

What the hell? Aiden thought as he immediately rolled off the injured man and felt the wind from bullets flying all around, impacting the snow and hitting the rocks, ricocheting and snapping. Aiden flung himself over both men just as the bullets stopped and he heard the massive roar of a jet engine shake the ground.

—

Josiah had no idea how long he had been at it. He'd just finished ordering another air strike; had walked each of three separate fighters in on multiple runs. He couldn't tell how many, a half-dozen? The rocks just kept firing at them. His analytical mind did a series of ghastly calculations. He estimated how many rounds of high explosive shells had been fired, seemingly to no effect. The Warthog circling around for another pass had plenty of bombs, but they were so close. *Should we start dropping bombs? Risk the proximity to end the fight and get us out?* Maybe he could have them level the trees and make that a new landing zone. *How long would that take?* The F-16s were out of rounds but were refueling and could come in to start dropping them. One of his men was dead, more wounded. *They don't have much time.*

—

Aiden looked up to see the dark shape of an A-10 Warthog pulling up and turning left out of sight. He looked back down and saw Ray was rolling over, onto his good elbow, still holding his rifle against his chest with the strong grip of his good hand. Matt wasn't moving. *Dammit, not Matt, too?*

Aiden grabbed Ray by the collar, turned and dragged the heavier man the rest of the way and dumped him down behind the rock. Without a word he went back and was on top of Matt, rolling him over and pulling his face out of the snow. Aiden swore out loud, and then prayed. *Lord, get us out of this soon.* Then Aiden began the mental calculations: all that needed to be done with Ray, how badly Dave was hurt, and what just happened to Matt? The Golden Hour. *Josey, we don't have time. You have to end this. Get us out of here.*

10

BEYOND

THE GOLDEN HOUR

21:45:00 EDT
US Special Operations Command, Florida

"Sir, the Chalk 2 chopper is repeating their PJs' request to be inserted at LZ Delta and move on foot to assist."

General DeBerg had already turned down their first request. It was too unpredictable. Any LZ on that mountain could result in another torn up chopper. Now, with nine men pinned down and under fire, casualties mounting, he was considering it.

The Chalk 1 chopper had limped back to base with a destroyed engine. Another was inbound to replace it, but the Chalk 2 chopper would have to break off soon to refuel in air, taking time that the men on the ground might not have. Everyone monitored the battle on the airwaves. There was also a quick reaction force of SEALs chomping at the bit at their base, ready to insert if ordered. Landing in a hot LZ would be the prerogative of the pilot. Authority to make the attempt was the prerogative of the general.

DeBerg had so much firepower in the air, surely it was just a matter of minutes until the enemy ground forces would be subdued enough to get a chopper in. Sending in more PJs could provide the manpower needed to take the enemy position by foot as well as minimize casualties, but there was no guarantee they would be able to land at LZ Delta, or get to LZ Charlie before it was opened. Then what?

They would have to move up to them on foot in deep snow, and find them while avoiding enemy contact themselves, then link up with Polaris — who were currently shooting at anything that moved — and coordinate and then engage with enough force to take an elevated and heavily fortified enemy position that a half-dozen fighter strikes for over an hour hadn't been able to make a dent in.

On the other hand, Polaris might all die within the hour without help. There were few good options.

"Negative. Hold their current position."

The general looked at the wall display, which showed a real-time image from a surveillance drone circling overhead. He watched another fighter fly through the frame, clouds of debris in its wake and he prayed, *God keep them alive somehow till we can get 'em.*

———

06:50:00
Afghanistan

Porter fired continuously while Josiah pressed the radio receiver to his ear and tried to communicate to the fighters overhead. *How much ammo does Porter have?* Enemy fire let up after every strafing run, but came back with equal or greater intensity a few moments later. *We need to start dropping bombs.*

It was so risky at this range. The reverberation, the shrapnel from exploding rocks, the fireball…a miss, the wind; all potential outcomes that were as likely as not when dropping a bomb this close to friendly forces. As a pilot he dreaded it. His greatest fear was always collateral damage. He trained for it, and had expertly provided close air support, never once hitting a friendly position, though many times he'd held his breath while pulling the trigger. In the cockpit he marveled at the desperation of men on the ground under fire who had such complete faith in the abilities of their fighter cover. These guys trusted them to hit their targets every time, even when that target was a stone's throw away, as it was now.

From the air, Josiah could never fully appreciate the desperation that caused men to rely on such risk. Now from the ground, he understood perfectly. Unfortunately for Josiah, he knew — as most ground troops did not— how hard it is to drop a bomb on target. The calculations rested on the skill of the individual pilot.

Josiah called up the A-10 pilot who was part of his own squadron; recognized the man's voice immediately. He requested a bomb to be dropped in pilot speak, grateful to be speaking with one of his own men, strangely comforted — despite all the bullets flying around him — by the familiar voice. "Copy that Captain, inbound."

"Bombs incoming!" Josiah shouted as loudly as he could.

The PJs and SEALs dropped down and covered their heads with their arms, all aware that bombs being dropped at this range could easily kill them all. As the bombs dropped free, Josiah could actually hear the metal canisters falling through the sky. Through closed eyes and quick prayers the men held their breath.

The impact shook the ground as the bombs fell dead on target and produced a massive shower of dust and snow, and for a moment it was quiet. Hope rekindled. *Maybe it's finally over. Maybe the chopper can land now.* They waited three long minutes wondering what the fate of the enemy was.

But the shots rang out again, the fire worked its way back into a steady repetition, and Josiah got back on the radio, spoke with the fourth fighter of the day, and wondered if he should risk larger ordnance.

———

Matt wasn't breathing and Aiden wasn't sure why. He tore open Matt's jacket and began pounding on his heart with the side of his fist. Then he began compressions and blew air into his mouth, no time to fumble for his breathing apparatus. It was old school mouth-to-mouth, just like he'd read about in the Boy Scout manual of his childhood years ago, and after several repetitions Matt took a breath and began to cough. Aiden rolled him over and did a blood check to see if there was a bullet hole or other injury that had caused Matt to collapse. Blood was oozing out of his ear.

Suddenly, as if someone had shoved a meat hook into his shoulder and pulled, Aiden was spun around. It knocked him off balance as the piece of lead planted somewhere in his muscle. It hurt like a bad cut, but he'd find out later. He ignored the pain and turned his attention back to Matt, who was crawling, trying to get his bearings. Aiden stepped up, grabbed Matt by the back of the collar as he rose and pulled him toward the rocks, flinging him down next to Ray who was trying to get his weapon turned around so he could use it. Aiden was about to tell Ray to lie down when he heard Teddy holler from behind, "Corpsman!"

Aiden turned and ran toward the shouting. Teddy was still shooting, Dave was down, Teddy had his rifle up on his shoulder but was leaning to the left, trying to get a hand on Dave's wound while still firing. Blood shot through Teddy's fingers, which were covering both of Dave's hands as he clutched his own neck. *Oh crap*, Aiden thought as he ran. Teddy moved over and put his blood-soaked glove back to the stock of his rifle and regained his aim. He never stopped firing.

Aiden whipped a bandage out of his cargo pocket, shoved it into the hole in Dave's neck and pushed as hard as he could on his artery. *Why are all the PJs getting hit? I need help.* Aiden looked over toward the flank. Gator and Hector were shooting toward the trees with their backs to Porter and Josiah.

"Hector!" Aiden yelled.

Hector looked sideways, his rifle against his cheek. He yelled something at Gator and ran, sliding into position next to Aiden, and instantly both were working feverishly to stop Dave from bleeding. A pool of red snow was under Dave's head and he was crashing from immense blood loss. Aiden ripped open a pack of bandages and shoved the mass of gauze against him. *More pressure. Hurry. We need blood.*

Dave, unconscious, released hold of his own neck,

allowing Hector to put in an IV and a bag of blood. He tried to hold it up but too many bullets were flying, and he had to crouch low alongside Aiden to try and stabilize Dave. Hector propped up Dave's rifle by the butt end and hung the bag of blood from the sight, hoping an enemy round didn't hit it.

"We've got to move him to the others," Aiden said. Hector looked and saw Ray leaning on his good elbow, bandaged bloody stump in the snow and looking through the scope of his sniper rifle. Ray was taking slow, carefully aimed shots every few seconds. Next to him lay Matt, who wasn't moving, but Aiden verified he was still breathing, just unconscious again. *Maybe Matt has a concussion, or maybe his inner ear is shattered?* Next to him was the body of Andy, covered with a blanket that Matt must've placed on him before passing out again.

Teddy covered them, picking off targets, swinging from right to left and back again. Aiden quickly glanced back to the casualty area, then back to Dave and saw Dave's eyes open wide, then begin to roll back, his pulse weak and diminishing under Aiden's fingers. He began pumping Dave's heart as Hector held the bandages, disregarding the sound of bullets registering in the back of his consciousness. *No. Don't quit, Dave.* After a moment he stopped and listened, holding Dave's wrist.

He was breathing. There was a slow pulse. Steady, but weak.

"Okay, let's move him," Aiden decided. "You lift his legs and I'll get his head. Not too fast or you'll rip out the IV."

With that, Aiden pulled up Dave and he and Hector moved backwards toward the casualty collection point, Teddy moving behind them to give cover. Hector steadied Dave's legs, draped the IV'd arm across his torso, and with no other option, held the end of the bag of blood with his teeth while trying not to trip in the deep snow. Somehow they got behind the blessed rock.

Teddy, kneeling halfway between where Dave had been hit and where Aiden and Hector had just taken him, seemed to be single-handedly holding off that entire flank. Hector hung the blood bag over the end of Dave's rifle, while Aiden updated him.

"Dave's the most critical. Keep an eye on him while I look over the others."

No sooner had the words escaped Aiden's lips than Gator shouted behind them, "Man down!" as he ran towards toward Teddy, but was himself knocked down by bullets slamming into his chest body armor. Aiden saw Gator fall backwards and roll over, then raise his rifle and return fire. Teddy was on the ground and not moving. Bullets flew everywhere, in multiple directions from multiple sources. Aiden took a breath and dashed off amid them toward the man on the ground.

"Bomb's incoming!" Aiden heard Josiah's voice from far off just as he skidded next to Teddy. There was blood all over his face but it wasn't gushing; he had taken a bullet to his left eye socket. Aiden felt behind Teddy's head expecting to find a hole and worse, but to his amazement the SEAL's head seemed perfectly intact. The bullet must be lodged in his eye somewhere.

Just then, the explosion from the bomb Josey had just ordered rocked the ground, spitting snow and rocks over both men. Aiden rose up wondering if it might be over. Ten seconds later, the shooting started up again.

"He alive?" Gator asked, unable to look for himself amidst the barrage of enemy fire.

"Yeah, but he's out.

Gator fired his weapon at the little black dots that kept poking up above the ridgeline "Hard to kill, huh?"

Aiden heard Gator say as he crawled in behind him, rifle up and shooting every few seconds. Aiden only grunted and looked back at Teddy.

Aiden took it all in while caressing Teddy's limp but living head in his hand. *We can't last much longer, Josey.*

"Cover me while I move him," Aiden said.

Before Gator could offer to help, Aiden heaved Teddy's 280 pounds — with another 80 pounds of gear and ammo — onto his shoulders, and stumbled up. Aiden was strong but this was more than he had ever lifted. He recalled hauling freshly cut tree trunks as a kid with his father. *Just get it up on your shoulder, and let your legs do the lifting,* his dad used to say. He had done this before, and he found that he could do it now.

He heaved the hulk of a man onto his shoulder and took the first grueling steps in the deep snow, stumbling and feeling the burning in his arms and legs, as well as the almost forgotten gunshot wound in his other shoulder.

Josey and Porter saw it out of the corners of their eyes and silently willed Aiden to move faster while also laying on more cover fire.

It felt like forever for Aiden to move two feet and the bullets continued to fly. He gained momentum and thirty seconds later deposited Teddy's massive frame with a thud and a spray of snow into the line of critically wounded men. Aiden was desperate for water but had to settle for a long breath. *How many now? How long has it been? You've got to end this, Josey.*

"Aiden, get down!" Hector yelled as he pushed Aiden into the snow. Another inaccurately fired RPG exploded behind them peppering Aiden with buckshot-sized rocks that tore through his back and shoulders. He felt the pain of the shrapnel, metal or rocks, he didn't know, but his attention immediately redirected to

Hector, swearing in Spanish, wincing in pain, lying flat and trying to roll over, but falling onto his back, sweating and slamming his fist into the snow.

"Lie still, Hector. Can you move your legs?" Aiden said, putting his hand up to his own neck and immediately bringing it back down again, as pain seared through a hundred little cuts on his neck.

Hector rolled his legs back and forth, raised his arms and nodded his head. He tried to roll over onto his elbow, got halfway up, and then collapsed again.

Through sweaty gasps Hector answered, "Yeah. I can move everything, I just can't get up off my back. Something is jacked up. I'm sorry, Aiden."

Nerves in his spine, Aiden concluded. *Probably a piece of rock or metal pinching one of his discs.* He'd have to be immobilized before something severed, paralyzing him. *I need a backboard. Don't have one. There's one on the chopper, the chopper that can't land because that damned hill just keeps shooting.*

Aiden looked over the casualties. Matt unconscious, Dave critical, Hector unable to stand; two of the SEALs, one shot through the eye and unconscious, the other missing an arm. They needed to be medevac'd an hour ago. *How much longer? We've got to get these men out of here. They're all going to die. We're going to die, unless... Josey, you have to end this.*

He looked back toward Gator, still firing, quickly but methodically. Then toward his brother and Porter, the SEAL hovering over the precious radio operator, everyone on both sides of the fight knowing full well that Josiah and his ability to call in air support was the only thing preventing a field full of dead Americans. Then, as Aiden watched, Gator fell backwards for the second time that day. This time he didn't get back up.

Aiden sprang back into the open.

Aiden ran at full speed once again across the gauntlet of bullets. Two bullets hit him in the calf and thigh and knocked him off his feet briefly; he got up again and quickly limped the rest of the way and landed on top of Gator. He tore open the SEAL's body armor and clothes to get to his chest, pulled off the layers of bloody shirts and fleece and got his hand up under his ribs and felt a long gash. Aiden reached back into one of his pockets for a bandage. He put pressure on the wound with one hand and tore open the gauze with his teeth. A bullet went through Aiden's collar and he fell forward.

He felt like someone had hit him from behind with a baseball bat. He was lying face to face with Gator and his eyes met the SEAL's, a man Aiden had only met yesterday, who shared his meal with him the night before, who found his brother hours before that. Now that same man was lying here, looking to the left, and he seemed to be sinking away with heavy, gurgling breaths. Gator was alert, but didn't seem anxious or angry. He had a vacant look, but was swinging his rifle a few inches off the ground as if trying to look through the scope, then dropped it as the strength disappeared.

I'm losing him.

He had watched this man fight for Lord knows how long, protecting fallen men, his fellow PJs, his brother, never once calling for medical assistance — despite being hit numerous times, as Aiden could see. His heart sank and he pushed aside the pain of his own wounds, and got back up on his knees.

———

Josiah saw Aiden get up, fully exposed yet working on Gator. *Aiden, get down,* he wanted to yell, but he was just then vectoring in another strafing run from another Warthog.

———

Aiden tried to lift his left arm and pain shot through his entire left side, but he found he could still use it. His hand was still on Gator's wound, and through clenched teeth he brought his left arm up and lifted Gator's body up to get his hand under him so he could wrap the dressing around Gator's chest while the Warthog bought them a few minutes reprieve.

If we can stop the bleeding and get Gator to a hospital, he might have a chance. The golden hour. How long can we keep him alive? How long has it been since that first SEAL lost his arm? An hour? Two? Three? Aiden had no idea. Now he looked at Gator. *You're not going to die on me. Not you, not today. None of them are going to die.* Aiden looked at Gator's drooping eyes. *No. Say something to him. You've got get him back. Say something.*

"Hey! Look at me, Gator. You're not quitting today. Don't you ring that bell!"

———

Gator heard the words as an echo through a canyon. His eyes were closed and he was somewhere else completely, sleeping, or dying, he didn't know or care. He heard the PJ screaming in his face, "Don't you ring that bell!"

Suddenly Gator opened his eyes, back in the present. He'd heard those words reverberating through his semi-conscious mind once before. Don't ring the bell. Whatever happens don't ring the bell. It was a reference to Hell Week on Coronado Island, when would-be SEALS are thinned out in training. Men who can't cut it must ring the bell in the center of the quad three times and add their numbered helmet to the line of others, a physical representation of men who would never be U.S. Navy SEALs.

Gator had endured every amount of government-sanctioned torture that the instructors could come up with to sort out the men who were prone to quitting from the ones who would rather die than do so. All throughout that week, he had been told over and over by the instructors that all he had to do in order to get some sleep, a warm bed, and some hot chocolate was to stand up and come ring the bell. All of his pain would be over. Gator wanted to ring the bell so badly; had been on the verge of doing so more than once, but every time, a small part of him got angry with the notion of quitting. He renewed his determination and once again set his preference on death before surrender.

Now he was in that place again, and all he wanted to do was close his eyes and sleep, but the faint words of the PJ triggered that anger again. He was on a mountain, hurt but alive. *Man up, you pansy, there's work to do. You'll have another mission after this one, so just get it done and go home.* Gator set his will, refused to ring the bell. If someone else rang it for him — if his time was up — he could live with that, but he would never ring that bell himself, and so he opened his eyes.

"Copy that," Gator said finally.

"Gator, stay with me." Aiden said while simultaneously slapping the side of Gator's head with his left hand.

"Yeah," Gator answered, annoyed.

"Don't you ring that bell."

Gator smirked, closed his eyes for a moment and

then replied while shaking his head, "Yeah, whatever."

"Hey!" Aiden yelled again.

"What?" Gator said.

"You'll see your girl again, okay? I've got you. Just stay down, all right?"

"All right, but shut up, though," Gator said.

A sense of humor. Good. Aiden thought. *He's got some fight left in him. Now if I can just keep him from bleeding out.*

"Just lie still."

Aiden kept his right hand on the wound, and despite the pain in his left shoulder was still managing to keep him alive. *How long can Gator make it?* he wondered. *How long can the others?* Aiden looked over to Josiah. His brother was holding the radio receiver in one hand, their grandpa's Browning in the other. Josiah dropped the radio receiver, letting it dangle by its cord over his elbow and put both hands on his gun. Josiah fired off three aimed rounds in careful succession. Aiden was impressed. His brother was awesome. Aiden was far away but he could see the look in his brother's eye. It had an intensity that Aiden had only seen in Josey's eyes once before.

They had been sitting in church the weekend after Josey had first returned home from the Air Force. The service was just about to begin when Abigail Coles walked in alongside Nelson Sharpe. Abby had been Josiah's girlfriend for as long as anyone could remember. They grew up together as family friends, they fell in love; but then Josey joined the service, had reasoned that he didn't want to face the possibility of leaving Abby as a military widow. To everyone's dismay he broke up with her and he regretted it every day since. And here she was, sitting next to Nelson. Josey stared at them with a fire in his eye that Aiden had found delicious.

Aiden had leaned over to his brother, "It's your life. But if it were mine I'd go over and do something about that."

Josiah didn't speak; just turned away and sat with that look in his eye through the entire service. When it was over, he immediately got up, walked straight up to Abigail before Nelson had even stood up, looked straight into her eyes and spoke something. Aiden never knew what Josey said to her. Josey never told him, but three days later Josey and Abigail were married.

Now, on a barren mountain in the ranges of Afghanistan, Aiden saw that look again in his brother's eyes. It wasn't hate, it was love. Josiah didn't hate the men he was up against, he loved the ones they were trying to take away from him. And so he fought them.

But Josey was losing, and so was Aiden.

There was no way to deny it any longer. They were losing this fight, would lose it in the end. There are moments in sports where you realize who is going to win and who is going to lose, and that the rest of the time on the clock will simply wind down toward the inevitable outcome. It was like that here. Aiden knew the math, the odds, the reality. They were all going to die. There were not enough Americans to beat them. There was not enough time to withstand them, not with these casualties. As a group they were slowly dying. No, that's not right. We're dying faster now than we were then. *Is there any chance?* Aiden looked at Josey. He looked at his casualty collection point. Then he looked down at Gator whose eyes were flickering. *There is no time left. You need to end it, Josey.*

"Josey!" Aiden yelled as loudly as his damaged body could manage.

Josiah didn't hear him. Aiden waved his arm at him and yelled again, louder, "Josey!"

This time Josiah turned toward Aiden, who was attached to Gator. He looked at his brother with those eyes, receiver in one hand, pistol in the other, motioned with his head a reply.

Aiden waved toward the casualty collection point. The men laid in a long row behind the rock, Hector crawling painfully among them checking vitals. Aiden yelled again, "They're all going to die! You have to end it!"

Then Aiden lifted his shot arm and through biting pain in his shoulder pointed toward the enemy position, "Level it! Whatever it takes!"

Josiah looked at his little brother. Aiden was obviously in tremendous pain. Josiah realized his brother was right, this couldn't go on. He felt like a failure. What was he doing? They were all going to die and he couldn't stop that, not like this. He realized it was just like kicking a hornet's nest, and getting stung over and over. *How do we kill hornet nests? We stomp it into the ground. Destroy it with one blow.*

Josiah nodded to Aiden and then got down behind the snow bank and made a decision.

"I need a JDAM. Who can assist?" Josiah asked over the radio.

Porter stopped and looked at Josiah for a moment, unsure what to make out of what he had just heard. A Joint Direct Attack Munition has two thousand pounds of laser- and GPS-guided explosives, and its effects are devastating. So devastating in fact, that using one when allied ground troops are close is nearly suicidal. Nonetheless, Josiah realized that it was the only option left.

He prayed that the pilot could hit the pickle barrel, because if he didn't…well, they would all be dead anyway. He needed Porter to lace the target first, though.

"Can you get up there and paint it?" Josiah asked him, pointing to a large rocky ridge behind them.

"Yeah, but stay down. I'll get up there," Porter said.

Porter needed to get higher in order to get the laser sighted onto the proper target. He glanced around and quickly settled on climbing up onto the packed snow they'd made their shelters from, some forty yards away. He dashed toward it, leaving Josey behind. He leaped up to the highest possible vantage point and aimed the laser at what he hoped was the center of the enemy line. Porter held the laser painted firmly on the target as bullets ripped through his body.

Josiah waited impatiently for the B-52 to confirm the laser signature. Now it came down to a number of factors: human calculation, computer software, wind and air density, topographical accuracy. Despite this, the JDAM nearly always fell within forty feet of its target. In this case, if it didn't, no one would be left to tell the tale.

The B-52 pilot approaching at forty thousand feet radioed to the ground, "Weapon release in five-four-three-two-one. JDAM away."

Josiah took a deep breath, they hollered, "JDAM incoming. Take cover!"

Porter could not take cover. He kept the laser pointed on target, knowing any slip might send the weapon off target.

Hector, surprised to hear the word JDAM, immediately looked around and then painfully threw his gun aside and himself over Matt and Teddy.

Aiden, still with his hand on Gator's chest wound, wrapped himself around him, cradled the man's head with his bad shoulder, and managed to cover most of Gator's upper body and part of his right leg. Aiden listened, and thought he could hear something humming through the air among the AK-47 rifle fire.

Then it impacted.

Aiden felt a rush of wind sucking him up and off of Gator momentarily, only to thrash him back down with such force that he felt like someone had slammed him in the back with a 2x6. His eyes closed instinctively and he felt snow envelop him and pelt him with ice and rocks. A wave of heat and stone and a roaring noise washed over him. An intense searing went through his right leg, followed by stinging wind and pain as a thousand rock fragments tore through first his clothing, and then his flesh and bones.

Aiden blacked out.

It only seemed a moment before he shook awake and pushed himself off of Gator. He saw Gator's eyes were still open and alert. Gator blinked and looked back at Aiden. Thank God, Aiden thought.

"You still with me, Gator? We're gonna get out of here."

For the first time in...hours?...Aiden heard silence. No enemy fire. He ventured to stand up to try and get a better vantage point and to see Josiah. Aiden lifted up off his left knee and brought his right leg around to try and take a step to lift himself up. When he tried to plant his right foot he immediately fell over and rolled away to his right and pain shot through his body from his ankle all the way up to the base of his neck. Aiden was stupefied. *What's the matter with me, he thought.* He tried to roll over and get up but Josiah was on top of him and threw Aiden onto his back.

"Just lie back. I got you."

Aiden looked up and around and saw the upside down image of Porter limping toward him and Gator. Porter paused at Gator, but then pulled out a package from his own left leg pocket and turned toward Aiden.

"Here, use this," Porter said as he handed the tourniquet to Josiah, and then fell onto his side.

Josiah unwrapped it and slid it over the stump that had been Aiden's right leg, blown away by the impact. Aiden lifted his head and saw the bloody mess absorbed into the pink snow. He lifted his head higher to try and see his casualty collection point but could only see Porter, bleeding from several places, and wanted to treat him.

Aiden, referring to Gator, said, "He's bleeding from the chest. You need to put pressure on his wound. Upper chest. His left side. Okay."

Porter had seen many amputees on the battlefield, but he had never seen one give clear and concise directions. Porter winced as he leaned up, found the wound and pushed on it. He looked at Gator and then looked around and was surprised that for the first time since dawn he didn't hear any shooting.

Then, to his elation, he heard a faint thumping. Helicopter rotor blades were approaching.

—

As soon as the chopper was two feet off the ground, fresh PJs were off the ramp running toward them. They reached the casualty collection point where Hector, crawling, gave them a quick orientation and run down of the casualties. Ray was first to go, then Dave, Teddy, Matt, and Hector last. In a matter of minutes each of the men were transported to the Chalk 1 chopper and were feverishly being readied for the long flight back to the nearest allied surgical hospital, every one of the Polaris and Raven operators at risk of dying in flight as the PJs worked to continue the care Aiden had started.

The Chalk 2 chopper landed nearly at the same time and took Aiden and Gator. They attempted to treat Porter but he waved them off and went to Gator's side. Josiah assisted and tried to stay out of their way as the PJs assigned him tasks, not the least of which was to take out a body bag and get Andy's body on board the chopper.

As they moved Aiden into the second chopper, Porter briefly locked eyes with Josiah, at his brother's side, and then they were gone.

Porter took one last look around, then limped onto the ramp.

On board, Aiden was still alert but his eyes were exhausted. He knew he had lost a ton of blood, but there was an IV in his arm and an oxygen mask on his mouth. He looked around the interior of the chopper to see what was going on, and could only see shapes of busy people, PJs mostly, huddled and doing what they do. Aiden noticed a mass off to the side, not being worked on. It was a long black bag covered by an American flag.

Aiden thought, How many more on the other chopper?

Josiah was sitting behind him. Aiden looked up and Josey just stared back. He didn't smile or speak. It was too loud to hear anything anyway. He just sat there with his hand on Aiden's head, stroking his short red hair for the first time since his mother had brought his little brother home, and Aiden didn't mind.

We're off the mountain. Your casualties are being cared for. There is nothing more you can do for them. You're done. Finally, Aiden had reached the end, and closed his eyes.

Vince Guerra

11

GATOR

Hampton, Virginia

I'm so cold. It's been freezing forever. I'm so sick of this. All I want is to be warm, just for a few hours. God, why am I so cold?

Gator painfully opened his eyes. His eyelids felt weighted down, or maybe crusted with something. He could see, but the image was fuzzy and distorted. He wondered where he was. All he could think about was being cold but his body didn't have the strength to shiver. He was cold in his bones, past his muscles and his skin. He had been cold like this once before but the memory was veiled. He tried to think of it, but his thoughts were scattered and he became confused again. He tried to raise his head to look around, gain his bearings, but his head wouldn't lift. *Where am I?* He fell asleep.

He opened his eyes again. *How long have I been here?* Everything was otherworldly. He looked around the room, slowly coming into focus. He saw fat, white, plastic equipment, monitors, and pale empty walls. The room was dim with some daylight trickling in from the window. He saw tubes coming from a metal stand down toward where he was lying, into his...

Hospital bed. I'm in a hospital.

How did I get here? Why am I here? Gator tried to remember what would have happened to send him to the hospital. *Oh yeah, I got shot, but...no, I've been home since then. I was home with Jen. I remember seeing her. We were back at our place. I saw the team, the Master Chief told me something, teased me. Porter drove me home.*

Images came to him in fragments. He could remember another hospital in Afghanistan, and a helicopter before that. He vaguely remembered a flight stateside, a commercial flight. He remembered watching part of a lame movie and then sleeping and being woken up by dinging noises and pain. *I was taken to a hospital, but not this one, not then? That was a different hospital. Germany, maybe? How many hospitals have I been in?* He couldn't remember. *How long ago was that?*

The more he tried to piece it together, the more confused he got, and the cold was biting him again, and his head— every inch of his body hurt. He was cold again and he tried to use his arms to bring the blankets in closer but he couldn't move his arms. He tried to roll over but the pain was too much to endure.

Gator had no strength. All he could do was think and feel cold.

He opened his eyes again and managed to lift up his head a little bit higher. He looked toward his feet this time, and saw someone sitting in a chair in the corner near the foot of his bed. *Who is that?* The man was holding a small wooden box.

Suddenly he knew. *Porter.* Porter was sitting at the

foot of his hospital bed, holding the box Gator had asked him to bring. Porter had brought the box to the hospital and handed it to Gator. Gator remembered holding it and looking at the treasure he'd placed inside it. He had looked at it longingly and sadly for a long time. Then, he had closed it and given it to Porter, and told him, "Give it to that PJ. Tell him thank you."

Gator didn't remember how long ago that had been. *Maybe it just happened. Maybe it was days ago.* Gator looked at Porter, noticed that he was sitting with his head bowed low.

Is he praying? Gator wondered. *I must be pretty screwed if Porter is praying.* Gator started to chuckle to himself, then the pain took over and he winced.

Porter was not the praying type. Gator's wife, Jennifer, and Porter had had it out over religion one night after a game of cards and the conversation had been fascinating. Only two things were resolved that night: Porter was an atheist, and Jen was not afraid to argue. Now here was Porter, appearing to be praying, and Gator wondered what would come of it.

Jen must be happy. He almost smiled, but then the realization struck him like a punch to the gut. *Jen. Where is Jen?*

He looked around and saw her. Her back was to him. She was standing on the other side of his bed, too far away for him to touch her even if he'd been able. She was standing in front of a window covered by slightly parted blinds. He couldn't see her face, but he knew it was Jen; he knew her from behind. A smile formed on Gator's face, then pain tore at his heart. He would have cried if he had been able to, but that would have required his body to have the ability to make tears, and his body was busy trying to keep him alive. *Am I dying? Is that why they're both here?*

Gator also recognized the old blue hoodie she was wearing. She was wearing it the night they met, on the beach, her first beach party as a freshman at the University of Florida. Back then he was a nervous eighteen-year old named Christopher, smitten stupid by the girl in the blue Florida Gator's hoodie and short black shorts. Christopher wasn't drunk, though the beer he just finished may have contributed to his determination to talk to the girl.

Fortunately for him he'd stopped at one beer, or else their story might have ended right then and there. Jen was not a drinker, had very little patience for those who were — patience that would be tested in earnest when she became the wife of a SEAL. But that was four years away. On this night Christopher flirted brilliantly, and Jen was impressed by the guy not holding a red plastic cup. Clear-eyed and gentlemanly, he won her heart that night, but she didn't tell him till after their next few dates, and a few kisses goodnight.

It has been worth every minute. *I love you, Jen. I wish I could tell you.*

Jen had been patient with her Gator, as she came to call him, along with his ROTC buddies — and she tolerated them, and his commanders, and eventually his SEAL fraternity, despite their rowdy type-A personalities. She especially loved Porter, though in an older-brother-who-regularly-pissed-her-off kind of way. He and Gator had become like brothers, so that made him her brother, too.

She was patient with Gator when he rejected her invitations to come to church, over and over again. She had patiently and passionately pleaded her case to him on all manner of subjects: salvation, vehicle purchases, career decisions (mainly his), wedding plans (mainly hers), and children. They had none. The tear in his heart ripped a little bit further.

She will never be a mother now. That's all my fault. Gator silently lamented. She had wanted to get pregnant for years. She was okay waiting when they were newlyweds. At that time she had just finished up her nursing degree and was waiting to see where the Navy would send him before applying to hospitals. A year later, settled in at Virginia Beach, she asked if he would be willing to start a family. He deflected the request – ostensibly, because it was bad timing with his training schedule and likely deployment to follow, but both of them knew it was fear. Fatherhood seemed the only thing that Gator had ever been afraid of. She quietly endured his lack of willingness. For the past year the elephant was always in the room.

The last time he was home she finally pressed the issue. They argued, nicely, but it had ended in tears…again. Gator's argument was always the same. What if something happened and he didn't come back? He didn't want to leave her a widow, a single mother. He was thinking of her, or so he justified it to himself. Now he realized the truth was the opposite. He would be dead anyway, and she would be left alone. She would still be a widow, but also denied the consolatory comfort of a child to cling to in her grief.

Gator realized he would never have a son or daughter to bear his name. Nobody would ever tell the child how their daddy had served his country, had fought for the lives of others, had made a difference. Great-grandchildren would never exist. He would simply end, and Jen would move on, he hoped. The Navy would eventually forget about her. *And I'm leaving her with nothing. I'm so sorry, Jen,* he wanted so badly to tell her. *You were right, again.*

Gator again tried to speak but had no voice. He

remembered now. He had been released from the hospital, and brought home. He and Jen had taken it easy for a couple of days. Being a nurse, she had known what he needed — mainly rest. No visitors, no phones, no video games, no college football. She had loved him for two days as he recovered from his third surgery on as many continents. *Then what?*

What Gator did not remember was how Jen had woken him up in the middle of the night; sweat was pouring off him in a desperate, massive fever, trying to kill the infection that had set in. Then came his collapse on the bathroom floor, and Jen trying to wake and cool him before the EMTs arrived to whisk him back to the same hospital. There had been little time to talk before that night, so few had been the nights back in his own bed. Now I'm stuck here, immobile, dying, and she's over there, looking out the window, thinking, probably crying.

I'm so cold.

He could only remember ever having been this cold once before, on his last day of Hell Week at the beginning of his BUD/S training on Coronado. So many men had already washed out during the grueling training designed to do just that. He and the rest of his remaining classmates had endured the wet and sandy Pacific shore nonstop, day and night, for days on end. They had ended their day hoisting rubber rafts back to shore and been ordered to lie down on the wet pier while trainers hosed them with freezing cold water. That was the coldest he had ever been in his life. The trainers had kept telling the shivering, blue-lipped men, "Just get up and ring this bell here, and it will all end." They had encouraged them, not tauntingly, but honestly, respectfully, "You'll get a warm blanket, and a cup of hot chocolate. You'll be asleep in a warm bed in ten minutes, just ring the bell."

The instructors had backed ambulances up to the pier and Gator had seen a man in the back of one, blissfully sipping from a Styrofoam cup, wrapped in a blanket with a pretty Navy nurse taking his vitals. Gator had wanted to ring the bell so bad. He had wanted to get warm; anything to get warm. He had almost gotten up, but either from a force of will he didn't know he possessed, or an angelic hand via the prayers of a wife miles away who daily interceded for his success, he had stuck his soaked white t-shirt to the cold wet wooden pier and endured the pain, the cold, and the despair, and become a United States Navy SEAL.

But that was a long time ago. He was cold again and he heard the voices again. "Just ring the bell, and you can get warm," they told him. But there was another voice he remembered. It was the voice of that PJ, Gator couldn't remember his name, but remembered seeing him running back and forth all over the battlefield. The guy was like a flash of lightening, had been there as soon as someone got hit. As soon as Gator went down he remembered that PJ on top of him, telling him, ordering him, "Don't you ring that bell! You're not done yet." He said it so many times that Gator had agreed just to shut him up.

But that PJ was gone now. Gator was here. Jen was next to him. He couldn't see her eyes. He had seen those beautiful eyes light up when she greeted him off the plane, broken, sitting in a wheelchair.

Thank you for that. Thank you for letting me see her again, he said silently to the PJ whose name he couldn't remember.

The cold enveloped him again, despair followed, the pain increased. Ice shot through his body and he wanted to scream but nothing came, just cold and pain.

I can't stand this. It's so cold. It hurts so much. God, help me.

And then he heard something else: the words of a song he didn't realize he knew. They shot straight and true and ministered to him, and his heart leapt and beat faster as it responded:

> *And on that day when my strength is failing*
> *The end draws near and my time has come*
> *Still my soul will sing Your praise unending*
> *Ten-thousand years*
> *and then forever more…*

Suddenly warmth began to creep up his body from his toes, like thawing ice, all the way to the top of his head. Light filled his closed eyelids, and peace overwhelmed his body, and joy filled his heart, and a smile formed on his lips.

And Gator rang the bell.

Beyond the Golden Hour

Vince Guerra

12

JEN

Washington D.C.

Jennifer Peterson, war widow, looked at the reflection in the oversized hotel bathroom mirror. The fluorescent lights were cruel and seemed to reveal every detail of her bloodshot, tired eyes. She debated changing out of her pale yellow dress into the black one. She had brought both, unsure what the occasion demanded, unlike the last such ceremony she'd attended, when black was the theme of the day, along with sunglasses covering teary eyes, dark Navy uniforms as far as the eye could see, and a procession of men, individually pounding a gold U.S. Navy Seal Trident into the lid of her husband's coffin. Each thud — a profound gesture of respect on their parts — had been like a series of kicks in her gut. She knew it was what

Gator would have wanted; had seen him do it too many times before, when she had been the one trying not to stare from across the way at the grieving spouse or mother being presented the folded American flag. It hurt. Maybe one day it would heal, but at the time it was all pain.

From the moment Gator slipped away in the hospital all those months ago, it was consistent, recurring pain. All the team guys who were there in the end, her pastors and their wives, her parents and Gator's parents rushed in from Florida, the nurses and doctors who shrank back into the shadows as everyone wept, or those who rushed off to pound on something in private — all pain.

And worst of all was Porter, sitting in silence the whole time with his head bowed, looking at the small wooden box in his hands. He never left Jen, though he never really spoke to her, either. He merely sat and waited. Porter's presence had been one of the few earthly comforts since that day. She always felt that if Porter was around, somehow, so was Gator. He escorted her through the formalities, through the ceremonies, to and from the gatherings afterward. He allowed her to swear, and break things in her despair in the solitude of her home, and she knew he had probably done so himself, though when he was with her he always showed silent strength from a respectful distance.

As the hours spread into months she clung closer to Jesus than ever before, and though the pain remained, she found she could sleep, and dream, and good thoughts slowly came back. She found joy in simple things she and Gator had both loved, like swimming, fresh seafood, and old movies. And though those things made her weepy, she continued to enjoy them all the more.

It had been like a furlough, a healing sabbatical, but now she was back in the world of military formality. She was going to the White House of all places, for an entirely different reason, and she was terrified of what would happen. Porter was there of course; she knew he was just outside her hotel room door, waiting to escort her once again. She looked again at the dress and decided to stick with the pale yellow; figured that maybe as long as she didn't wear black nobody would recognize her. Perhaps she could put on the fake happy smile and slip in and out of the Rose Garden, complete her mission for Gator, and get out without having to wear that war-widow badge again.

For a few moments she considered feigning sickness or some other excuse. More than once Porter had encouraged her to do so. He'd offered time and time again to deliver it for her, but Jen had determined it was her right to bestow and hers alone. She and Gator had been one flesh, and if anyone was to represent his last wish, it would be her.

Maybe it would be good — it was, after all, The White House— and despite the intense heat it was a beautiful spring day. And more than that, she wanted to meet him. There were so many words she wanted to speak, thoughts to convey. She'd started so many letters to him, each time tearing them up or balling them into the trash, or the floor next to it, where they'd lie for a week or more.

No, today was the day. She would wear her pretty yellow dress, and don her dark sunglasses, and smile in the White House garden with Porter watching over her, and sip water or tea, and make her presentation, and then get the hell out of there.

Vince Guerra

13

UNCOMMON

The White House, Washington D.C.

"There are many things in the modern world which can be, and rightfully are defined, as courageous. Some acts, however, stand a cut above the rest, and are performed by men and women in unimaginable circumstances with uncommon valor and uncompromising resolve. The young man here today is one such as these…"

Aiden had been entirely uncomfortable that day in the White House Rose Garden, partially because of his still-recovering injuries, partially due to the stifling Virginia summer heat he was forced to endure in full dress uniform, but also because he just didn't want to be there. It was hard to accept a medal for enduring a series of tragedies that seemed to mount as the days passed.

"Not every man on that mountain was fortunate enough to come back to us. Air Force staff sergeant Andrew Bell, combat air controller, fell on the field of battle. Senior airman Jason Holmes, flight engineer, and petty officer Christopher Peterson, Navy SEAL, likewise succumbed to injuries sustained on that awful day. There are, however, five men who are alive today as a

direct result of actions undertaken by the man we choose to honor. That Others May Live. It is the creed of the Air Force's elite unit known as pararescue..."

Aiden didn't hear the rest of the President's speech. He was lost in thought from that point on; simply wanted it to end as soon as possible so he, his parents, and siblings could all get away from throngs of sweaty men in expensive suits vying to have their picture taken with him. Aiden endured the rest of the ceremony as graciously as he could. He smiled and kept his composure as he was brought up to do, but bit his lip more than once when confronted with absurd questions. He knew this was part of the show, and what was expected of him.

After a half-hour or so the crowd began to thin, and Aiden began looking for an opportunity to finally break away and leave. He caught Josey's eye in hope of finding approval to cut out. Josey's wide smile and polite chuckles were betrayed by his eyes, pleading for Aiden to shoot him.

The Suits — as Aiden had come to call them in his head — seemed to be about finished with Josey. The brothers gestured to each other that it was time to leave when Aiden noticed a civilian woman in a pale yellow dress moving from around the back corner of the garden directly toward him. She seemed to not want to be spoken to; didn't want to be there any more than he did, he could tell.

She was beautiful. She was also sad. Her hair was in a ponytail, and her sunglasses were on top of her head, and she was holding something. She seemed unsure as to whether or not she should approach, hesitating, but Aiden was sure she meant to speak with him. He smiled an invitation at her, then noticed she was accompanied by a Navy officer who looked familiar. Then their eyes met. She froze.

The young woman took a deep breath and began to walk to Aiden with obvious determination. As she got closer, Aiden noticed her magnificent eyes; they penetrated him and made him nervous. He and Josiah recognized Porter standing protectively and silent behind her. Without introduction, both brothers knew instinctively that this was Gator's widow, and they were at a loss for words.

Aiden's mouth was dry. His mind searched frantically for something to say to her. He was dumbstruck, paralyzed with fear of saying the wrong thing, overwhelmed with his own emotions, attempting by sheer force of will to hold back tears and to keep from shaking. Porter's firm countenance offered no levity. He was there only as a pillar, a support for conducting a meeting that was not about him. Porter gave them a subtle nod of recognition, and then looked down at his best friend's widow, putting a steadying hand on the small of her back.

Jennifer Peterson held out her hand. As she took Aiden's, she looked into his eyes. It didn't occur to her that Aiden might have no idea who she was, or who her husband was. She had lost the clarity to consider introductions. She had planned out what she was going to say a hundred times in the mirror. She was going to be strong, gracious, and encouraging. She was going to tell Aiden how much Gator had admired and respected him, how much he had wanted to meet him again and convey his gratitude. Jen had planned it all out: the introduction, presenting the gift, a joke, even. But as soon as she looked into his eyes, everything failed her, and tears welled up in her eyes, and all she could do was blurt out with a cracking voice, "Thank you."

And then she began to sob, uncontrollably from her

gut. Her right hand, still holding Aiden's, went limp; she brought her other hand, still holding the box, up to grab Porter to steady herself. Porter came in close to support her, but before he could do so, Aiden's mother was there, seeing the woman's grief and loving her in an instant. Jen did not hesitate as she turned toward the older woman and wept. Mrs. McCoy stroked her hair and gently patted her back as the three men in full dress uniform were completely undone, and had no words. There were no words.

When she was ready, Jen, still holding his mother's hand, turned back to Aiden and continued with a stronger voice. "Thank you…for allowing my Gator to come home." The long pause was a deafening silence.

She held out the box to him. "He wanted you to have this. He said to say thank you, and that he was sorry." Aiden took it from her and she turned to walk away, but instead turned back and hugged him. Aiden couldn't speak, and simply hugged her back as tenderly as he knew how, in the manner one hugs a delicate great-grandmother, afraid of breaking her. Jennifer let go, and with Porter, walked away.

—

It was Tuesday night, and quiet; the docks were somewhere to their right and the air was salty. Josiah and Aiden walked down Vista Circle, Virginia Beach, and were as relaxed as either of them had been in months. The city was unfamiliar to both of them so Porter had offered to pick them up at their hotel, but the brothers wanted to walk. They wanted to pretend they were normal for a while, and had already endured too many escorts in the past several weeks. Still, they wouldn't turn down this invitation for the world.

"Had to wear the Air Force hoodie?" Aiden teased Josiah. "I hear these guys throw down faster than the 70's Flyers."

"Meh, I'll just hide behind you."

"You always did on the ice anyway." They laughed, and saw the sign on the street.

"This is it." They turned right, and crossed the parking lot into a dockside oyster bar.

They walked in and before they could find Porter they were greeted by a huge hulk of a man they instantly recognized, but not by the scar across his odd-looking eye.

"Make way for the zoomies!" Teddy hollered, startling several customers. "But watch out for this one." He motioned to Aiden for the men at his table. "He once tossed me around like a rag doll."

Aiden and Josiah shook Teddy's aggressive hand in turn, and then went around the table giving introductory nods to chiseled, tattooed men they'd never seen before. All except for one, a black man missing his left arm.

"Ray," Aiden greeted, "I was hoping you'd be here."

"Wouldn't miss it, once I found out Porter was paying," he laughed.

"Sure, you can order from the kid menu, RayRay. They got plenty of Coors for you," Porter replied. "But for my favorite flyboy here —" Porter thumped Josiah so hard on the shoulder he winced "— and his kid brother over there, money is no good. Keep your wallet in your pocket or I'll have Teddy throw you off the dock. Now, Captain," he looked at Josey. "About that beer."

EPILOGUE

Aiden swung the axe and got the satisfying snap of a perfect split; two pieces flew off in opposite directions. He took a breath and stood up straight, stretching his back, examining the pile for the next log. He grabbed one a bit larger and set it on the block, turned it slightly to find the best angle, and swung again. With a jarring thunk, the blade stuck deep in the center of the thick, damp log. He frowned, jiggled the handle, then leaned on it, putting the palm of his other hand on the edge of the bark to leverage it out. It was in there good. After a few grunts and lunges he managed to wiggle it free, and set it up for another swing.

This time he brought the head down even harder, slightly toward the edge, and it snapped cleanly in two. Take that, Bessie.

Aiden smiled and looked toward the sky, and the billowing clouds around the mountain's edge. Winter was coming soon but the air still smelled like fall. Someday soon he'd walk outside, and the air would have a chill that indicated frost. Tires would need to be changed, garden hoses would need to be drained and coiled up, and snow would come. But not yet. He still had time to get this pile chopped before the snow flew.

It wasn't his wood — this was his parents house. Aiden was at home for a few weeks. Josey was back overseas on another deployment.

Josiah had gone through the usual inquiry: the investigation into the cause of the sixty-million-dollar A-10's crash, the medical and mental evaluations along with the reviews of his after-action performance, as well as his decision-making both in the air and on the ground in the hours following his ejection. It was a grueling uncertainty that gnawed at Josiah and Abigail for weeks.

In the end, not only was Captain Josiah McCoy cleared of any fault, but he was commended for his leadership, action, and decision-making. He was promoted, which meant he was sent back to his squadron, which meant he was sent away from his family and back to the war, because the United States needed men like Josiah who could fly those sixty-million-dollar aircraft and save lives on the ground. And America needed him doing it right away.

Aiden heard a small airplane overhead and instinctively looked up, thinking of his brother half a world away. *Keep it in the air this time, Josey.* He turned his attention back to the woodpile. He still had a couple of cords to go, but he didn't mind. He had begged his dad to let him chop wood as a young man, and took it on as his task ever since. He had been curiously uncertain in his ability to do it now, after everything that had happened. He approached it as another in his series of challenges. So many things that used to be simple were now challenging, yet he discovered each new task he tried could be accomplished one way or another.

He learned he could run five miles a day on his prosthetic leg. He could also swim. His nephew referred to it as his Darth Vader leg, which Aiden loved. He wasn't the type of guy to dwell on it. He could still chop wood, he could still do a lot of things. He just couldn't be a combat pararescue jumper anymore.

That was what brought him back to the wood pile today. Chopping wood let him think. It provided perfect clarity, and there were plenty of things to think about, including a decision he'd been wrestling with for months.

Back when he was lying in a hospital bed in Maryland, recovering from his first surgery stateside, his father walked into his room, freshly flown in from across the country to see him for the first time in a year. At the sight of his strong, determined son in a hospital bed with a bandaged stump where his leg used to be, Aiden's father was speechless. His dad was rarely at a loss for words, but Aiden could tell he was worried about saying the wrong thing; had always been cautious with his speech toward his children, his greatest desire being to build them up and encourage them. But how does one encourage and build up a young man who, after displaying such courage and skill in combat, suddenly found himself incapable of ever doing it again?

Aiden sensed the hesitance in his father's eyes and mercifully decided to break the ice. His father always told him there were two types of men in this world: the Shoulda, Woulda, Coulda guys, and the What Next guys. The Shoulda, Woulda, Coulda guys pined over the past, what did or didn't happen, or what might have happened, if only. They were miserable individuals trapped in a prison of their own design, who rarely ever succeeded except by chance, and usually squandered their success in short order. The What Next guys, on the other hand, were responsible for most of the victories throughout history. Great leaders were of the latter stock, and if you wanted what they had, you had to follow their example.

With this in mind, Aiden looked up at his dad, and half-smiled. "What next? Huh, dad?"

Mr. McCoy, not the least bit surprised by his son's confidence, tried to stifle the tears welling in his eyes as he replied, "That's right, son." He gave him a long hug and they both wept. But from that moment on, Aiden never looked back.

What next? Aiden had wondered since that day, and still didn't have an answer. He would never again be a combat pararescueman. Having only one leg took that off of the table, but there were plenty of options available to him within the service. He could remain with the PJs as a training officer in a number of schools. His skills and his experience were invaluable, and everyone in the upper echelon knew it. He had his choice of assignments, but he found few of them appealing. He wanted to be in on the action.

He could go into medical school. He groaned at the thought, still loathed the prospect of a lecture hall. Firefighter was out, but perhaps private EMT, he'd been told. It was something else to think about.

And then there were the offers that came out of left field. Publishers were asking him to write a book about the famous battle and his part at the center of it. He had been bombarded with offers from high-end speaking engagements to school assemblies, appearances at sporting events, and conferences in large cities for organizations he'd never heard of. Talk shows on television and radio wanted interviews. He was annoyed by it and had ignored most of it, capitulating initially to a few of the local press outlets out of what he felt was a responsibility to defend the truth of the account, but he quickly clammed up when the experience somehow made him feel ...dirty. He had almost ignored the call from an ex-president. He was honored but felt like a bumbling fool.

That was months ago, and the publicity had died down but he still had a decision to make. Aiden went back to chopping wood with greater concentration, listening for direction and the confirmation of what he should do with the rest of his life.

He didn't consider himself a war hero — though everyone else did, even Josiah, whose opinion he normally relied upon. The gold star fixed to the end of a blue ribbon is the nation's highest military decoration, as revered as it is rare. Aiden was honored to have been awarded it, but he didn't particularly care for the item itself. He felt undeserving, but not in a self-loathing way. He simply felt he had done his job, and others had perhaps done more. It was kept in a beautiful case on a wall at his parent's house. Everyone who visited the home admired it. Aiden never did.

In quiet hours, Aiden remembered that awful morning. His nightmares were few and far between now, but the memories were as vivid as yesterday. He didn't fear them, they propelled him. In those moments he would find himself going up to his bedroom desk. There, on a shelf was a small wooden box hardly anybody ever noticed.

Only Josiah was ever shown its contents. It had been given to him in the Rose Garden of The White House. Not by the President or any dignitary, but by the delicate woman in the pale yellow dress who had summoned the courage needed to honor her dying husband's last request, and fallen broken into the arms of Aiden's mother, who had tenderly held her and stroked her hair as if she were her own daughter. Aiden would open the box to remember, and to pray, and though he never touched its contents, he would look at it for a long time, admiring the intricate design, the rarity of the thing itself, and become overwhelmed by the knowledge of what it took for men to receive it. And somehow, he would find healing in doing so. It was a golden eagle, perched on an anchor, with a pistol in one talon and a trident in the other. It was the SEAL Trident, the emblem pinned on the lapel of each new SEAL after completing the training which began an even more demanding and grueling career — a career that would too often end with such tridents adorning the caskets of its recipients, if not for the uncommon people who make getting home possible, that others may live, even if only long enough to tell the ones they love goodbye.

Vince Guerra

ACKNOWLEDGEMENTS

There are, of course, so many people who make something like this possible. I would like to give a special thanks to Rachel and Mike at Full Spectrum Editing for the technical assistance, to Jake at Crystal Clear Creative for the enthusiasm over the cover design project, and for Kendra at LaCroix Photography for making my awkward smile, nice. Lastly to my wife Shannon, who has encouraged me every step of the way, though at her request, I will edit my own gore from now on.

Vince Guerra

ABOUT THE AUTHOR

Vince Guerra is a writer living in Wasilla, Alaska. *Beyond the Golden Hour* is his first novel, and the first in a four-book series.

You can find his writing, and information on upcoming projects, including sequels at vinceguerra.com.

Sign up for weekly email as vinceguerra.com/allies

Vince Guerra

CPSIA information can be obtained
at www.ICGtesting.com
Printed in the USA
LVHW04*1836091018
593004LV00001B/2/P